# *What a Girl Needs*

## AIMÉE DUFFY

Harper*Impulse* an imprint of
HarperCollins*Publishers* Ltd
77–85 Fulham Palace Road
Hammersmith, London W6 8JB

www.harpercollins.co.uk

A Paperback Original 2014

First published in Great Britain in ebook format by Harper*Impulse* 2013



A catalogue record for this book
is available from the British Library

ISBN: 978-0-00-759168-8

This novel is entirely a work of fiction.
The names, characters and incidents portrayed in it are
the work of the author's imagination. Any resemblance to
actual persons, living or dead, events or localities is
entirely coincidental.

Automatically produced by Atomik ePublisher from Easypress

# AIMÉE DUFFY

All my life I've been dreaming up stories. My mum said when I was little I used to make all the My Little Pony figurines talk to each other and even fall in love. Later, it was Barbie and Ken. In my teens, I played matchmaker with my friends at school. When I wasn't creating imaginary scenarios, I had my nose stuck in books, reading across genres and there was one thing I loved more than the escapism—the fact a story could touch me so deeply, like I was experiencing everything along with my characters. I knew from early on this was something I wanted to do for others.

Fast forward a few years and the dream almost got lost in real life, but I still couldn't shake it completely. Now I write sizzling romance with the hope of making my readers' hearts race as if they are falling in love for the first time.

*I definitely need to dedicate this one to Susan Thomson. The conversations we've had will keep the ideas flowing for years!*

# Chapter 1

*Dear Sally,*

*I read your column weekly but never thought I'd be writing this email. The truth is there's something wrong with me. I can't climax. I've never been able to, and my recent ex told me this was normal for some women. Not the women I know. Was he telling the truth? Sometimes it feels like I'm the only one.*

*Yours,*

*Anonymous*

Georgia Lewis forced herself to leave it at that. It was one thing to think of herself as a freak, another to sign off using the label. Moving the mouse over the mat provided by Briggs Department Stores, she tried to click 'send', but her finger wouldn't obey the command.

Frustrated, she let go of the mouse and raked a hand through her hair, pushing it out of her face. She couldn't be the only woman in New York who'd never experienced what her friends kept banging on about, could she? Plus she'd created a false email address so none of Sally's Sexual Help readers would know it was *her* who sent it in, so what did it matter?

She needed to pull on her big-girl panties and send the damn thing. Maybe then she'd be able to concentrate on the end-of-year accounts on her desk. After all, she was here to work, not worry about body parts that didn't function correctly.

Resolved, she reached for the mouse again. Her desk phone rang and she stifled a sigh. Abandoning the mouse, she picked up the phone.

'Accounts Department,' she answered, though she could hardly call it that, more 'two women forgotten in closets at the back of the building.'

'Georgia, I need the buying accounts for last month.'

His deep voice made her skin prickle, like it always did. She shook off the weird sensation. He was her new boss; until his father got better anyway, and she'd never let herself look at him any other way. Okay, maybe she had on occasion, when she trailed behind him in the hall. Who wouldn't check out an ass like his? It was high and firm and utterly squeezable.

'Sure, Maxton. I'll get them ready.'

'Georgia…'

She rolled her eyes. 'Max. Sorry.'

Hard to break a habit of a lifetime. His father, Maxton Briggs the First, never allowed his name to be shortened.

But it was Maxton Briggs the Second running the show now.

'You'd better. I'd hate to have to punish you.'

He disconnected the call leaving her staring at the receiver. Heat rose in her cheeks and her heart hammered in her chest. He didn't mean…

No, he didn't. He was joking. God. She had to get a grip. Sexual frustration was driving her to think her boss was flirting with her. And sure, Max was less formal than his father, and she supposed a good guy to work for, but since his break-up, which was unfortunately witnessed by half the staff at Briggs, he wasn't his usual happy-go-lucky self. Not to mention a little bit weird. Though she couldn't blame him for that.

She rose so quickly she left her swivel chair spinning. Pulling open the cabinet drawer, she shuffled the slings until she came across the empty one which should have housed the file he wanted.

'Damn it.'

The sooner she gave Max the file and sent him on his merry way, the better. Usually she struggled to keep her thoughts from rolling off her tongue around everyday people; with him around it was impossible. And the boss didn't need to know what she thought of his ass, or how hot he looked in one of those charcoal suits with the silk ties. Or even about those dreams she'd had starring Maxton the Second, and very little in the way of clothes.

Well, apart from his ties. The silk ones, though, he never wore them as such. Either they were around her wrists securing her to her bed frame, or sometimes she dressed in nothing but a tie and pair of skyscraper stilettos.

A flush spread over her body, flooding into her lower tummy and making her shiver. Shit, she had to stop thinking about ties. None of it was knowledge she wanted to share with him.

*Girl, the file. Get the damn file.*

A quick glance around the hole she called an office didn't help. Loose papers and an old coffee mug hid a desk she remembered was mahogany. Stacks of blue files were piled in a corner next to a half-dead plant. The file she was looking for was beige. On top of the filing cabinets? She hadn't touched that area in a year and the inch of dust confirmed it.

Then it clicked. She'd left it with Janice to double-check the final reports.

Taking off at full speed – for a woman in five inch stilettos anyway – she bolted next door. Janice was on the phone, twirling a lock of her permed shoulder-length hair that was now more gray than brown. Her mentor blew a bubble of pink gum while she nodded, even though the person on the other end of the line couldn't see her.

Georgia crossed the room and stabbed the bubble with her super-sharp new manicure, catching Janice's full attention. She mouthed 'buying accounts' and, thank God, Janice knew what she meant. She rummaged around her equally cluttered desk for what felt like an age.

Georgia briefly wondered if she had a mentor who was organized, she'd follow suit, but quickly dismissed it when an image of her unruly bedroom popped into her mind. Thank God her roommate Eloisa had OCD when it came to cleaning or their apartment would never be fit for company.

Janice mumbled what sounded like an agreement into the phone while she located the file. Grabbing it, Georgia called a quick 'Thanks' over her shoulder and she was off again.

Her journey back was frantic, especially since she noticed the empty hall. The water cooler two doors away was usually circled by the gossip crew come three-thirty, and their absence made the hairs on the back of Georgia's neck stand to attention.

Oh, but it was much, much worse than she could imagine.

When she got to the doorway of her room, all six foot four of male glory was already on her chair, facing her computer with a frown above his deep-blue eyes. His dirty-blond hair was neater than usual, swept away from his face, but the waves made her think of him rolling out of bed after he'd just run his hand through it. Or worse, like she'd just run her hands through it, pulling him down into a kiss that would melt her panties.

*Quit it. He's my boss.*

But then the blood drained from her face, leaving it numb. Her whole body froze as she stared at him wide-eyed, comprehension slamming into her mind. Who'd have thought mortification could paralyze someone? Not her. Until now.

She forced herself to unfreeze and took a step into the room. Pulling on her best 'what the hell are you doing?' glare, she cleared her throat.

Max straightened and turned to her with his full lips parted.

Georgia refused to let herself look at his mouth and focused on being mad—completely ignoring the fact she'd been using working hours, not to mention the company's internet connection, to try and fix her sex life. Or current lack of one. After all, no guy wanted the ego beating of bedding her.

'What are you doing?' she demanded. But she'd never live the shame of this one down. Her boss now knew she was a freak.

Max stood, ran a hand down the front of his suit to smooth imaginary wrinkles, or because he was stumped at what to do. He cleared his throat, but before he could say a word, Georgia took control of the situation and shoved the file into his hands.

'Everything you need is in there, now if you'll excuse me I have work to do.' And shame to live down, but she could do that without an audience thank you very much.

'Georgia—'

'Don't.' She shook her head, fighting back the burn creeping up her neck.

He eyed her for what felt like an hour, studying her with an intensity that made the blush spread. She cleared the way to the door and headed toward the filing cabinets, hating the attention he was paying her. Especially now he *knew*. God, a man like him, all virile male with testosterone seeping from every one of his pores, was the last person in the world she'd want to think she was a freak.

The door to her office clicked closed and she heaved a sigh of relief, which turned into a squeak as she turned around to see he was still standing there. He'd ditched the file on top of a bunch of papers on her desk, and had his arms folded across his chest. The delicate material of his suit jacket pulled tight over trim muscles, and she had to force herself to focus on his face.

'There's nothing wrong with you,' he said.

'Excuse me?'

But she'd heard him and understood what he was referring to. Eloisa had often been in predicaments she'd described as so embarrassing she wished a hole would open in the ground and suck her in. Georgia had never understood, since nothing normally embarrassed her, and if she started to feel uncomfortable she took herself out of the situation. But right now, with nowhere to run—unless she wanted to climb out the window and take her chances with the two-story drop—and all of her failings as a woman laid bare for her boss, Georgia understood her friend's words perfectly. She'd have to grit her teeth and get through this, showing as little emotion as possible. And bite her tongue. The last thing she needed was her runaway mouth making this a hundred times worse.

Why the hell had she left that email open?

'You heard me.' Max thrust his chin in the direction of the computer and her cheeks caught fire, or felt like they did anyway. 'What kind of jerks have you been dating?'

Anger leaked into his tone and she wondered if Mr. Mood Swing was paying a visit. She squared her shoulders. 'That's not your business. None of this is.'

One brow rose over his incredulous eyes. 'When you use company time to worry about your sex life, it becomes my business.'

Georgia's quick tongue deserted her. He was right, she should have waited until she'd gone home, but Eloisa or Shey could have caught her, which struck her as horrifying. This situation made her friends' teasing seem like lying in the bath with her favorite scented salts after a hard day.

He took a step closer and she had to force herself to meet his eyes. They were stormy-blue now and focused on her in a way that made her blood race faster. Was it anger? Or something else? Closed into the crappy closet that acted as an office with him was unnerving, especially when a line formed above his brow and his jaw clenched tight.

Georgia's heart kicked up double time as she imagined a formal warning coming. Maybe he would even can her on the spot. Was what she did a violation of her contract? She couldn't remember.

Biting back her pride, she said, 'I'm sorry, it won't happen again.'

Both brows shot up this time, and his arms unfolded. Messing up that wavy hair of his with a drag of his hand, he blew out a breath. 'That's not why I'm pissed, actually. I'm pissed because a selfish jerk made you feel like there was something wrong with you.'

His eyes softened and she felt the pull of their connection right down to her toes. This was not what she was expecting. Her heart sped again but it had nothing to do with fear of losing her job.

'This is going to sound crazy.' Max's gaze dropped to the floor for a second, and the frown was back. When he looked at her again, determination etched across his handsome face, making her stomach swarm. 'I think we could help each other out.'

'I don't understand.' But she was starting to, though maybe that was wishful thinking. No, she shook the unruly thoughts away. She had to work with him, for cripes sakes.

His jaw tightened. 'I'm sure you heard the rumors after the Halloween party.'

Georgia nodded, remembering walking past the gossip circle down the hall where they had all whispered that Max's ex, Clarissa, was all over some guy dressed as Dracula, though she hadn't bothered listening to the specifics.

'She's with him now. He's one of our designers.'

His voice was void of emotion and his expression a mask. To hide his pain at losing his love, or maybe his anger at being betrayed, Georgia didn't know.

Max took a deep breath. 'My father still controls what designers we sign. As you know he likes to treat them to nights out to keep them from giving up their work to the competition. Since his health's deteriorating, I'm expected to play host at the parties.'

Georgia felt some of her own shame drain out of her, to be filled with a sad understanding. If the guy brought his date, Max's ex, he'd be forced into their company again. 'I'm—'

He held a hand out. 'I don't want your pity, I'm telling you because you could help me out on that score.'

Her brows furrowed. 'How?'

'Come with me to all the social events. As my girlfriend.'

Georgia's lips parted on a gasp. 'You can't be serious.'

It was clear from his tone he was dead serious. 'In return I'll show you that you *are* normal, that you can—'

'Stop.'

The shame burned back, along with something else that made her lower belly warm and tingly. She covered it with her hands, hoping to quell the sensations. No such luck. Especially when she'd just been imagining herself with him, doing all those things and more. That was fantasy, though; this was reality and it could never happen.

'You're my boss. That would be…'

Insane, delicious, even more embarrassing when he had solid proof she was a freak, and yet seriously tempting.

'Inappropriate, I know.' He stepped closer again and she backed up, knocking over the night-of-the-living-dead plant in the process. 'But it would benefit us both.'

His gaze got hot, then dipped to her mouth. On reflex she licked her lips, but cursed the second she did. She wasn't encouraging him. No way. Even if her panties were soaking at the thought of him dropping to his knees and hitching her skirt around her waist.

She couldn't let herself think about being with him. Couldn't allow the fantasy to form – well, this new one anyway. Shit, shit, shit.

Grasping for anger, she said, 'Let me get this straight. You want to save face in front of your ex and pay me in sexual favors when really, the only one getting anything from that would be you. I'm nobody's free hooker. Go find yourself another woman who'll pant all over you.'

Screw the fact he was supposed to be her boss. He'd crossed the line first.

Max took a step back, surprise widening his eyes. 'Georgia, I don't see you like that. I never have.'

'You've never *seen* me. Not as more than an employee.' She slammed her mouth shut before she gave away anything else to this man.

Frowning at her, he picked up the file. 'That's bullshit Georgia, and you know it.'

She pressed her lips together and glared at him, fighting the urge to open her mouth and let far more than she should roll off her tongue.

He let himself out, but before he closed the door behind him, he threw over his shoulder, 'This isn't the end of the conversation.'

'You'll get the same answer every time,' she let slip.

His slow grin made her heart stutter. 'We'll see.'

* * * *

Georgia was the third wheel. Again.

Shey was laughing at something Calvin had said, but Georgia wasn't focused much on their conversation. She was too busy pushing the pasta around her plate. Max's proposal earlier was playing on her mind; building up a storm of burning emotions she could only assume was anger.

'Georgia, you okay?' Shey asked.

She wanted to snip back with, *what do you think?* but bit her tongue. Everything grated at her since she got home to find Calvin teaching Shey how to cook. They looked disgustingly happy, with huge grins and puppy-dog eyes, as they moved around the kitchen.

Which was her first cue that she was not feeling like herself. Shey's happiness made her happy, or it usually did.

Damn Max for offering his stud services. Damn her for wanting them.

She could only imagine what he was like in bed. His body was built, could probably give her the best work-out of her life. All power, ego and sex on legs. It wouldn't make a damn bit of difference, though. He couldn't make her come, no man had and she'd lost hope a long time ago any of them could.

'This pasta's really good. He'll make a decent cook out of you yet,' Georgia said, hoping Shey would drop it.

Calvin glanced at Shey, then turned to her. 'Do you want me to leave so you two can talk?'

Georgia's throat got thick, and she tried to swallow against it. Calvin understood how close they all were and she knew he would go home if that was what she needed. Which, regardless of how much Shey loved Georgia, would make her friend unhappy. With Shey's new job, the couple hardly had much time together as it was.

She tried to dial her pissy mood down a notch. 'No, stay. I'm sorry.'

The lovebirds shared a look that said they didn't buy it. Georgia's skin prickled with irritation, but she ignored them and skewered a hunk of pasta. Forcing it into her mouth, she made herself chew, barely registering the oregano or tomato flavors.

What the hell was she going to do? Work was going to be more than awkward, especially if Max insisted on having that conversation again. Though the thing that played on her the most was the way he told her she'd been wrong that he'd never looked at her.

And she had to admit she'd noticed, but it had been so much safer thinking she was imagining it. Better for them both if she was the only one having hot and heavy dreams about Max swiping all the crap off her desk and taking her there, or against the filing cabinets, or even in the changing rooms of the store.

'Georgia, spill it. You look like you want to pounce on something.'

If only Shey knew.

Her friend's golden eyes burned with determination as she waited for Georgia to say something. Both her roomies knew her well enough to know she'd never lie, and they also knew her too well to be led astray by evading their questions.

Seeing no way around it, Georgia shrugged. 'Something happened at the office today. With my boss.'

'The one with the hot ass?' Shey asked, and was admonished by a glare from Calvin. She patted his hand. 'Her words. You know I think yours is—'

'Woah, too much information, Shey. I think my pasta's about to take a return trip.' Georgia was only half-joking. She'd heard more than enough on their Friday nights out when Eloisa and

Shey wouldn't shut up about all the amazing kinky sex they'd had. Which Shey was still having.

Though he'd been smiling at Shey, when Calvin turned to Georgia his expression was serious. 'He isn't harassing you, is he?'

Georgia thought about what Max had said. It was inappropriate, sure. And, well, a little insulting. And oh so very tempting. But he hadn't pushed, hadn't made a move to do more. She was certain that after she put her foot down with enough force to snap a spiky heel, he'd back off.

'No. He propositioned me.' Her stomach tingled just thinking about it.

'How?' Shey asked.

Georgia sighed. 'He asked me to be his… fake girlfriend, with all the benefits.'

Shey's chin dropped, but she recovered quickly. 'I don't get it. Why fake?'

That was something she hadn't asked herself until now. 'I don't know.'

Could he still be hung up on his ex? Maybe he thought having Georgia at his side would make Clarissa jealous and take him back? And as a way of saying thanks he'd have a go at making the woman who'd never had an orgasm come.

A shudder ran through her and her stomach turned over.

'You can report him for sexual harassment if this gets out of hand,' Calvin said.

With the frown he was sporting and his clenched jaw, Georgia guessed he'd like to do a lot more than make a complaint about him.

Shey squeezed his arm. 'Trust me, Georgia can look after herself. Right?'

The last part was directed at her and she nodded, but wasn't sure if it was the truth this time. Calvin's frown deepened, obviously he didn't agree with his girl.

'She's right. Maxton Briggs the Second isn't any different from other guys who've been on the end of a tongue lashing from me.'

But none of those other men had been her boss and Georgia hadn't wanted them like she wanted Max. No, she wanted to give him a different kind of tongue lashing altogether. Damn she had to stop fantasizing like this. She had to be proactive, had to think of a diplomatic way to deal with this. Thank God Eloisa walked in then, because if anyone knew where she stood in situations like this it was the newly qualified attorney of the house.

Georgia told her friends the full story.

# Chapter 2

As Georgia made her way to Max's office the next day, she was resolved to stop him from pushing her before it got out of hand. Last night she'd stayed up late with the girls and Calvin. She now had a plan of attack.

Offense was the best form of defense, after all.

Max's PA frowned when she entered the hall, but Georgia didn't stop. She walked right past the desk, making a beeline for his office at the far side of the lobby. Her heels clattered on the polished wooden floor. The place was big enough to host a pitch-and-put tournament, unlike the cramped hole she'd been shoved into, and that just annoyed her more.

'You can't go in there!' the woman trilled.

Georgia heard shuffling, then footsteps but she didn't spare the woman a glance. Her stomach was bubbling with the thought of opening his door, seeing him, and having her plans crash and burn. Arguing with his PA would only give her more time to chicken out.

She pushed his door wide and stormed right in. Max was on a call, grinning at something the other person had said. Her heart stilled as she took in his black shirt which was rolled up his forearms, silver tie knotted loosely and his wavy hair pushed back from his face.

*Oh hell.* She could just clear his desk right now, lie down with her legs spread and ask him to give it his best shot. He'd never looked so casual and relaxed, yet so completely fuckable that everything flew from her mind and her body revved up for his.

His PA was beside Georgia in a heartbeat, then urging her back out the door with a hand on her forearm. Georgia snapped out of her daytime fantasy and glared at the woman. She took a step back.

With an apology, Max ended his call.

'I'm so sorry, Mr. Briggs. I couldn't stop her.'

Nothing would have stopped her. Except maybe busted knee-caps, but his PA was too meek to dare.

'It's okay, Lucy. Leave us and close the door.'

'But Mr. Briggs, your next appointment is due soon.' Lucy wasn't giving up.

His smile was easy, like this happened to him every day. 'Tell them I won't be long if they arrive before this meeting's over.'

The way he looked at her, like he was down with the plan to screw six ways till Sunday on his desk, left no doubt in her mind about how attracted to her he was. Georgia had to swallow hard and lock her shaky knees so she didn't abandon her plan there and then and jump straight on him.

Lucy frowned at Georgia before she left. Maybe barging into his office wasn't the best idea she'd had. With little to no sleep the night before and her body vibrating with nerves all morning, she didn't want to put this off any longer. Only thing was, now she was here the perfectly polite speech she'd practiced dropped out of her head, like she hadn't spent an hour going over it, in front of a mirror, to practice keeping the bitchy out of her expression.

Instead all she could focus on was his throat and the flash of skin showing where two buttons had been left undone. A hot flush spread up her neck, and also down, until the tingly feeling in the pit of her stomach came back.

'Something I can help you with?' he asked, his eyes flicking down her body.

She fought the urge to tug at the hem of her skirt – though

whether to hike it up or down a bit, she didn't know.

'What you said yesterday—'

'Take a seat.'

She did, on one of the chairs at the other side of his desk. Not because he'd told her to, but because her legs had started to shake and sitting would be the safer option. 'Yesterday when you—'

'Look.' Max held his hands up.

Her eyes narrowed and again she had to keep her mouth shut before she said something she'd regret. Eventually. Maybe.

'It came out wrong, okay? I didn't come to ask if you wanted to start a fling,' he said, his expression serious.

Great, now all she could think about was that he didn't really want her and her lungs cramped. She sucked in a few breaths until the jerky movements faded. 'What did you mean?'

Max raked a hand through his hair. 'I did want you to come to the late summer ball with me at the end of the week, and it would be a bonus if you agreed to pretend to be my date. But when I saw the email I wanted to choke all the bastards that had treated you like a blow-up doll and I lost my head.'

Georgia frowned. He'd totally blown her out of the water. Especially now that it sounded like… 'So you thought offering a few pity fucks might sweeten the deal for me?'

She slammed her teeth shut with a clatter and her gaze dropped to his desk. Eyeing the stapler, she wondered if it would clip her tongue to the bottom of her mouth. Maybe that way she'd be forced to think before she spoke.

'Georgia.'

His voice dripped with command and she couldn't not meet his eyes again. They were hard, just like his expression. Shit, she'd gone too far. Then his tone changed again.

'You're very beautiful. From the first day I came here and saw you get out of that little red car, I wanted you. Then you leaned in and kissed that…' Max's jaw tightened. 'Guy. I was pissed off because I was attracted to you and I had no idea if you were serious with the guy. I tried to keep away as much as I could after that.'

She couldn't do anything except blink at him. To have him say he wanted her…

Her heart was going too fast, pumping hot blood around her body, including the inappropriate parts. She had to squeeze her knees together, but it didn't stop the pulsing between her legs. He'd no doubt used that low, seductive tone on purpose, probably knowing it made women melt. Well, she was damned if she'd let him see the effect it had on her; she was nobody's pity ride.

She'd never been this turned on, or pissed off.

'Knowing you're single now makes me want you more. And I know you want me too. It's pointless trying to deny it.'

She had to stop her jaw from dropping. The arrogant, condescending, pigheaded *ass*. There was no way he could know what she felt. *She* didn't know what she felt.

'How can you be so sure of yourself?'

Irritation bubbled just under the surface. She knew this conversation was getting dangerous, because her hand itched to slap that self-assured smirk right off his face.

'I know when a woman's checking me out. And right now? Your cheeks are flushed, your pupils are dilated and you're squirming in the seat like you need something between your legs. It's obvious you want me.'

Max spoke the words with such confidence, she wished she could force the lie out that she'd never thought of him in that way.

What the hell was she doing anyway? She was here to end this conversation for good, preferably in a way that meant she still got to keep her job. Briggs wasn't exactly her dream, but she was left alone to get on with her work. And it had perks, like the huge discounts on the amazing clothes and shoes. She never imagined fucking the boss would be a perk she couldn't have.

Still, it was time to say what she came here to. 'What you said yesterday was inappropriate and offensive. It crossed the line and broke sexual harassment laws put in place for a reason.'

The smile slipped and his expression hardened. His blue eyes glinted like chips of ice and she shrunk back into the chair. Not because she was scared, but because she was suddenly melting on the inside, wondering what hot angry sex with him would be like.

Would he tear her blouse open, popping the buttons? Rip her skirt right up the slit for easy access? Bend her over the desk, teasing her with his fingers while he pounded into her, pushing her toward her first-ever orgasm? Her clit throbbed as her lacy panties soaked through.

Forcing herself back to reality, she realized it would probably be the same as sex with any other man. A huge bitch-slap colored with disappointment.

'I won't harass you, Georgia, but I will have you in my bed. That's a fact, and not just because I want to fuck you so bad. You want me, too, and you need a man who isn't a selfish bastard.'

'*Please*, you have no idea what I need.' She meant the words to slice through him, but her ability to castrate a guy with her tongue had deserted her. His comments made her breathy, almost pant, and she squirmed a little at the way heat arrowed right between her legs.

The smile came back. 'I know exactly what you need.'

Max rose, then rounded the desk. He hauled her to her feet by her shoulders, but despite the speed he moved her it didn't hurt. His palms were gentle cupped around her arms and he pulled her close. A glance down was all she needed to see how hot he was for her. How much he really did want to fuck her. A little wordplay and he was half-mast. Her lacy boy shorts were soaked.

She had to pull back and not just because he was her boss. In the scheme of things, that didn't matter. Max would know if she faked it. He didn't seem the type who needed his ego stroked with her moans. His was so inflated with over-confidence she had no doubt he knew how to deliver on his promises. What he was suggesting they do was too tempting.

But it didn't mean he could get her off. She was strong, despite the way his proximity screwed with her senses. And she had her pride. Maybe she wouldn't be a pity fuck, but she would just be a tool for him to face off against his ex, or maybe even get her back. Georgia would just be a screw to fill the gap.

*Hell. No.* Max's place was solely in her fantasies, where he could almost make her come with just a look. That way was safer: it meant he'd never know how much of a freak she was.

She pushed out of his hold and knocked the chair over as she backed toward the door. 'Sex doesn't do anything for me apart from burn a few calories. I work for you, but that doesn't mean you can treat me like an easy lay.'

His jaw ticked and his eyes flamed in a way that made her want to go to him, drop to her knees and ask for instructions. Maybe unzip his fly, take him into her mouth so hard and fast he'd see stars.

Jesus, what was wrong with her?

'I'm beginning to think nothing about you is easy.'

She reached for the door handle, needing to get out before she crossed his office and let him do all the things he told her he would. Her body was alive with something hot and dangerous, something that made her want to lash out, give it to him hard, just to see him punished.

Which cooled her off. Where was all the insanity coming from?

'You're right, I'm a contrary bitch. Remember that next time you try to tell me what I need.'

Georgia was out of his office before he had a chance to reply. She slammed the door behind her and headed for her hobbit hole, ignoring Lucy's startled expression. Her legs were shaking, her whole body trembling, and she had a flush like she'd just come down with a fever.

'He's wrong, he's so not what I need,' she muttered as she stormed down the corridor to her office, scowling at the fact she couldn't even lie convincingly to herself. She slammed the door of her cubbyhole closed and slumped against it with gritted teeth.

Adrenaline ripped through her veins alongside a whole truckload of pissed off. Not to mention the fact her body was vibrating, almost begging to be touched.

Georgia grabbed the hem of her skirt and tugged it around her hips. She wasn't gentle about sliding her hand into her panties, less so about parting herself and rubbing her fingers over her flesh. She was soaked, burning hot and the little nub had swollen. But all the rubbing, all the building, went fucking nowhere. As usual.

She stifled a scream and righted her clothing. How the hell did she expect any man to make her come when she couldn't get the job done herself?

* * * *

They both needed time to calm down and Max had given it to her. Two days had passed since he'd contacted Georgia, despite the fact he'd wanted to go straight to her office, lay her down on the desk and teach her a lesson they'd both enjoy.

Again he'd made a mess of asking for this favor, which was seriously screwing up his plan to pay that bastard Marcello back. If he couldn't convince everyone he'd moved on from Clarissa – despite her rubbing her new relationship in his face, when it came time to drop Marcello the other designers could get antsy and walk. If Georgia could just pretend to be besotted with him for a few functions, that's all it would take.

The end-of-summer ball his father had organized for his precious designers was fast approaching and the perfect chance to put his plan into action. As he pulled up outside, Briggs decided to use a different approach with Georgia that might get her to agree.

Time to turn on the charm. Something he'd long since lost patience for. Public humiliation would do that to a guy.

On the way through the store, he practiced a little on his staff. The sales women returned his smiles with a chorus of *Good morning, Mr. Briggs*. By the time he reached Georgia's side of the building, with a coffee one of the girls had given him on the way, his smile came easier, though he knew he'd have to freeze it in place for this meeting.

Georgia's door was open, but he didn't barge in. Just as well since she was bent over an open drawer in the filing cabinet. A dart of heat bolted south and he gritted his teeth. Now was not the time to be appreciating her curvy ass covered in cream silk. Even if he could imagine it without the threads. Blood pounded into his cock and he had to take a deep breath to fight the barrage of arousal.

Shit, had it just been too long since he last had sex, or was it knowing she was available now – at fucking last – that made her more attractive?

Max knocked on the door. She straightened and whirled around. His breath caught as he took her in from head to toe.

Georgia always had an elegant beauty about her that stunned him every time he saw her. Today it was the cream silk clinging to every slender curve of her body, the way her hair, curling slightly at the tips, fell loose around her shoulders, the understated make-up enhancing those huge green eyes, and her deep-red pout that when parted against her wrath could almost bring him to heel.

Maybe it was the fact she dressed like a lady and he wanted to screw her in his office, with her fire and anger and unhidden lust.

Her eyes narrowed and she folded her arms across her chest. 'What do you want?'

Max made sure the charming smile was still in place and stayed right where he was. Any closer and he'd want to touch her. 'To apologize.'

Her lips parted and for once Georgia Lewis seemed lost for words. His smile was easier to hold as he spoke. 'I was an ass. I shouldn't have said those things to you.'

She let her arms fall to her sides, but he didn't miss the way she squared her shoulders.

'Before you say anything, I want to clear something up.'

This time he did enter the room, then closed the door. Suspicion tightened her expression, but he only leaned back against the wood, keeping space between them. Last thing he needed was one of the big-mouthed sales assistants hearing this.

'I didn't suggest you pretend to be my girlfriend in exchange for sex because I felt sorry for you. I hadn't meant to say it at all, but the second I read your email I wanted to be the guy to show you what you've been missing. Call it my inner caveman taking over my mouth.'

Though she looked bewildered, she opened her mouth to say something. No doubt give him hell. He held his hand up.

'Let me finish. It was inappropriate and not the way your boss should behave. If I didn't think you were interested I wouldn't have said a word. The thing is, whether you want to accept that part of the deal or not, I'd still like you to come to the ball with me tonight. I'll pay you overtime, will even let you pick whatever dress you want from the store and I won't push you for anything else. You have my word.'

Her throat worked and he ignored the shiver that ran through him wondering what it would have felt like if she'd done that around his dick. Hauling his head out of his pants, he focused on her frown, hoping that didn't mean she was about to shoot him down again.

The thing was, he needed her to do this for him. Though he'd caught Georgia eyeing him up in the past, he'd never gotten the same vibe from her as he had from other members of staff who were attracted to him. There didn't seem to be a needy bone in her body, and that was perfect, because a real relationship wasn't something he wanted again.

'I don't understand why you can't ask someone else. I doubt you're hard up for a date.'

Her cheeks flushed with pink and he fought back a laugh at her admission. 'I don't want to ask anyone else. There's no one I can trust to do this. You come in every day, leaving your personal life at the door. Well,' He cocked a brow and she shuffled from foot to foot, remembering the email, 'most of the time you do. I never see you gossiping with the others and you're stunning. How could I not ask you?'

Max couldn't believe how easy it was to say all this to a woman. He hadn't dated since Clarissa, but being with Georgia was different. There was attraction, but not one she wanted to act on. Yet. But that was all there was between them. No pressure, no risk of falling hard and being rejected. Just pure lust.

And he knew she felt the same, so he wasn't going to give up hope they could have a little fun. Friends and colleagues with benefits and clear boundaries. And he'd make sure he left her satisfied every time..

Finally, she spoke, 'I'm not sure. I'll need time to think about it.'

The smile froze on his face. 'It's tonight.'

Her glare would have had a weaker man bolting out the door. 'Friday's girls' night.'

He held his hands up at her clipped tone. 'Look, think about it. Like I said, you can take whatever you want from the store and I can pay you overtime. I'm only asking for tonight.'

She folded her arms again, but her expression smoothed a little. 'And the next function? That's in a fortnight isn't it?'

Yeah, and there were also a few dinners and shows in the upcoming weeks, but he didn't need to freak her out by telling her that now. 'Let's just see how tonight goes.'

Her jaw tightened. 'I've not agreed to go.'

Max decided not to push further, but left her with something that may tempt her. 'I have a meeting I need to get to. If you decide to come, email me and I'll let the sales girls know you're coming down. Sky's the limit.'

Excitement glinted in her eyes and she pursed her lips like she was trying hard not to smile.

'I'll let you know soon,' she said and the excitement was there in her voice too.

Since he was ninety percent sure she'd go with him, he decided it was time to leave before he said anything to get her worked up again. He opened the door, stuck his hands in his pockets and turned his back to her. He looked over his shoulder to see if she'd taken the bait and caught her staring at his ass with her lower lip trapped beneath her teeth. He wanted to grin, wanted to tell her she could have all of him if she wanted it, but forced himself to leave.

Max had no doubt he'd have Georgia where he wanted her. He just needed to tread carefully.

# Chapter 3

'I can't do it,' Georgia told her friends.

Eloisa's eyebrows almost hit her hairline. 'You've got the dress, the shoes, the clutch and the jewelry. I don't think he'll be thrilled if you changed your mind now.'

Georgia looked down at the midnight-blue dress. She was worried her skin would look too pale in poor lighting, especially since she was a week late on her spray tan. She'd been tempted to get one on her lunch hour, but orange wasn't sexy. Pity the tinted moisturizer hadn't done much but give her a light glow.

But that was the least of her worries.

A car was due to pick her up any minute to take her to the ball and she was sweating off all her make-up.

'Georgia, you agreed to go. If you'd told us first we could have talked you out of it, but you never said a word.' The look Shey threw her made her feel like a spoiled brat, getting everything she wanted then deciding she didn't anymore.

Which was pretty much true.

Georgia hadn't told them until she got home. Max had been so unlike himself that she'd believed he wouldn't push her, which had put her on a downer until he'd dangled pretty clothes bribes in front of her. She'd been excited about the prospect of shopping in Briggs with no price cap, and really what was one evening for

24

a dress that cost more than she made a month? And there was more than that; she got the matching shoes and accessories any girl would forego her hairdryer for.

After doing a mental inventory of Briggs' stock, there weren't many functional brain cells left to think about ulterior motives. The doubt hadn't kicked in until she left work and bumped into Max getting into his car. He'd winked at her and told her he couldn't wait for tonight, but it had sounded way too suggestive.

It had all clicked into place for her then. He'd told her a load of bull so he could get her to go with him. Get her exactly where he wanted her, then turn on the sexy. It was getting harder and harder to resist him, but she would. After all, it was only one night…

Shey topped up Georgia's wineglass and she swallowed half in one go. The buzzer sounded and she said, 'Don't let him in. I'll meet him downstairs.'

'You need to put your foot down with him,' Shey said. 'Unless…'

Georgia turned on her, 'Unless what?'

'Come on Georgia, you go on and on about how hot he is. Maybe fucking him will put you off him for good.'

'And you said he was pretty clear on what it would and wouldn't be, so there's no real risk,' Eloisa added.

Great, now they were both ganging up on her. Georgia stormed over to the door, snatching her clutch from the coffee table and handing Eloisa the glass as she passed. 'You're both idiots.'

'We love you too,' they chorused.

The buzzer went off again but Georgia didn't wait for it to be answered. She took the elevator down and used the time to compose herself. She may want him, but not enough to embarrass herself further by sleeping with him. Whatever his agenda for needing a date to these functions, she'd treat it like she would any other day in the office. He was her boss, whether she stood by his side or not.

So by the time she strolled through the marble lobby, she was resolved. At least until she opened the door and got a load of Max in a tux. She thought there was nothing hotter than Max in a charcoal suit, with one of his silky ties and his hair all askew – not that it was neat at the minute – but this was worse…Much worse.

The black suit hugged every inch of him, highlighting every bit of delicious sculpted muscle. His waistcoat was a deep purple and the shirt beneath was black too, not white. The effect it had against his tan skin was so hot her heart even missed a beat or two, but it didn't stop her blood from sizzling.

His eyes were stormy blue as they raked her over. 'How the hell do you expect me to keep my hands off you when you look like that?'

Best. Compliment. Ever.

Georgia couldn't help her grin any more than she could help her attraction for this man. She wanted his hands on her, right here, right now. Pity that wasn't part of the deal tonight. Although…

Feigning nonchalance, she strolled past him and climbed into the open door of the limo. Instead of going in the other side, he watched her shuffle over to make room for him. When he was inside and had given the driver instructions, Georgia turned to face him.

'Who says you have to keep your hands to yourself tonight? I'm playing the part of your girlfriend after all.'

A small frown pushed a line between his brows, but then he smiled, grabbed her around the waist and hauled her across the leather seat. Georgia gasped. The feel of his warm palms against her hips made her skin tingle. Though the chiffon was in the way, she almost felt naked pressed against his side. His crisp, cool aftershave invaded her senses and when he lowered his head to whisper in her ear, his breath caressed the nerves on her neck, making it hard to breathe.

'You've no idea how much I'm looking forward to it,' he said, then his lips brushed her earlobe, the touch scorching a fiery path down to her clit.

This close to him, all she could do was fight for control for the rest of the journey. She wanted to straddle him – hell, she was *that* ready. Maybe suggest they ditch the party and go straight to his place. She forced her mouth closed and bit her lip.

Max took her right hand in his, brought it over to rest on his solid thigh and rubbed teasing circles in her palm. She could feel the touch throbbing through her system, to every pulse point she had. Georgia knew it was dangerous to let him keep this up, but she was helpless to move, especially when he trailed his fingers down her forearm in light, teasing sweeps. A shiver ran through her and she focused hard on breathing.

'I should give you free reign in the store more often,' he said.

Georgia had to work to keep her voice even, but looking up at his smoky eyes didn't help her cause. 'Why?'

Max lowered his head until his lips were a few inches from hers. The air sawed out of her lungs and his minty breath brushed her face. She wanted him closer, wanted to know what those full lips would feel like against hers.

'Because you look heartbreakingly beautiful tonight.'

Her breath caught as his head dipped, but he didn't take her mouth. Instead his lips brushed her jaw, light as a feather, making her skin feel too tight and her mouth feel neglected.

'*Max.*' She whispered the word, but desperation leaked through.

He pulled away, which was *not* what she'd been begging for.

'I'm sorry, Georgia. I know I promised to keep this professional, but it's not easy.'

His expression was tight and his eyes almost dark gray with his need. The same need making her body vibrate and ready itself for him to take her. She pulled her hand back and slipped across the seat, ignoring his small frown and the protest screaming deep in her bones. Tonight wasn't about sex. Ten minutes and she'd already caved to him. She used the space to go over why asking him to slide up the privacy screen and fucking him where he sat would be the worst idea ever.

'Let's just keep the touching for when we're in public, okay?'

After all she couldn't lose control at the party and straddle him – she didn't want to end the night with them getting arrested.

He nodded once, then turned to look out the window at the city around them whizzing by. Georgia didn't look away, pretending to admire the same view of the buildings and streets all lit up in the fading light, but she didn't notice much. Instead she focused on his neck, so thick and strong. And his shoulder, which wasn't over-the-top muscly, but had perfect definition. She guessed he spent more time swimming than pumping weights. Then a vision of him doing a push/pull with naked arms and legs through water kicked up her body temperature and she forced her head to turn around.

Staying out of his bed was going to be harder than she thought, especially since she'd given him free reign to touch her at the party.

* * * *

The second they entered the function room, Max pulled Georgia close against his side. It was packed already, with Briggs' designers their dates and from all over. Tonight was different, though. It was the first of these functions he'd attended with a date since the split with Clarissa.

He waited for the usual anger to come, the vengeance against that bastard who'd seduced her right under his nose, but it didn't. All he could focus on was the woman pressed against his side and how she'd reacted to him in the car. Looked like this attraction between them had more perks than he'd thought.

'Your father knows how to throw a party,' Georgia murmured.

Max had to agree, though personally he thought it was over-the-top. A buffet prepared from the best gourmet restaurant in town was spread out at the far side of the ballroom and he had no doubt it would still be there at the end of the night. With the models in attendance, no one ate much. Although the champagne feature next to it would be sucked dry in an hour or so.

Already the live musician hired for the evening was singing, filling the room with an almost hazy sound. People had taken up space on the dance floor, but there were more seated at the tables scattered around the hall.

'Do you want something to drink?' he asked.

Georgia nodded, but he didn't guide her to the champagne feature. Instead they crossed the room to the bar. As they waited to be served, Max leaned against the wooden frame and pulled her closer until she was standing between his legs. She surprised him by slipping her hands under his waistcoat, spreading her palms over his abs.

Every muscle in his body hardened and blood pounded to his dick so fast the room swayed a little. She pressed their hips together. He gritted his teeth against the need to grind against her to get more friction, knowing that would cross lines she wasn't ready to cross yet.

Though by the dilation of her pupils and the flush spreading over her face, she wanted him just as much as he wanted her.

Max tried to think clearly with Georgia pressed against him, but it was tough. Why was it different for her now, when she'd pulled away in the limo?

'Don't you like champagne?' she asked.

Her words barely registered, not when he was picturing them alone, and all the things he'd do to her beautiful body. 'I prefer something harder.' And he needed it right about now.

She cocked a brow, a little smile playing around the corners of her mouth. A mouth he wanted to claim, right before he claimed every other part of her. He tugged her closer, his hands pressing against the top of her firm ass. Despite how toned she was, her breasts and stomach were soft against his chest and erection. He almost groaned.

'Like gin?' she whispered.

Max couldn't believe she could still keep up a conversation when he was using every ounce of his control not to drag her out of this party right now, maybe into the alley next to the hotel and take her hard and fast.

But he forced himself to play whatever game she had going. 'Bourbon.'

Max glanced toward the bar and saw the bartender was finishing up serving a couple in front – an underwear designer he thought was called Melissa and her date. 'What would you like to drink?' he asked Georgia.

She took a step back but he pulled her closer. When she glared at him, he explained. 'If you move now people will see more of me than they bargained for.'

Her skin flushed a pretty pink shade. 'Oh.'

He ordered their drinks, after she requested champagne, then moved her over to a table close to the bar. Sitting down was a must at this point. Though he didn't mind Georgia seeing how much he was feeling her, the rest of the guests didn't need to know.

She slipped in next to him, their backs against the wall and both scanned the crowd in silence for a minute. He should mingle, play the role of host his father usually did, but that wasn't going to happen for a while. He took a swig of his drink, then relaxed back into the chair.

It seemed the tent in his pants was a permanent fixture. He needed a distraction. 'Have you always lived in New York?' he asked her.

Georgia swallowed a mouthful of champagne. The way her slender throat moved didn't help his current situation.

'No, I grew up in Jersey. After my mom died I left town and went to university in the city. Haven't looked back since.'

Shit. 'I'm sorry, Georgia. I didn't know.'

She shrugged, but didn't meet his eyes. 'It was a long time ago. My mom was the only family I had until I moved here and met Shey and Eloisa. We live together. They're like the sisters I never had.'

All this time she'd worked for him and he had no idea she was an orphan. He'd never have guessed, not with the side of herself she fronted to the world. He took her hand on top of the table, wanting to offer her… something. He knew how hard it was losing a parent. And he was about to lose another. Her strength gave him hope that there was life after loss. Pity his father couldn't see shit the same way. 'That must have been tough.'

She smiled at him, but her eyes were sad. 'It was, but she was older when she had me.' Georgia shrugged. 'She was still too young to go, not even sixty yet, but Mom had led a happy life. Even if my dad hadn't been around. I miss her, but know she wanted me to make something of my life. Leaving Jersey and moving here was all because of her. She taught me how to survive.'

Admiration for her warmed him up in a different kind of way. She made it all sound so easy. Even though she lost the only family she had, Georgia picked herself up and moved on because she knew it's what her mother would have wanted for her. Yeah, his father could definitely learn a thing or two from her.

'How's your father doing?' she asked.

Max turned to her. Genuine concern creased her brow. After her confession, he found he wanted to share some of himself with her. 'Not good. He's been getting worse since my mother died.'

His next drink was harder to swallow. Since he was a kid his father had always told him there was nothing in the world that compared to meeting the woman of his dreams and spending every day of his life worshipping her.

But then when she passed away, his father might as well have too. He didn't think he had anything to live for, not even the business. Why the old man still insisted on overseeing the parties was anyone's guess.

It was like his life ended the day his wife took her last breath and every day since he was hopeful that he was one step closer to being with her again.

It wasn't healthy, and after Clarissa Max knew how wrong his father had been. A guy needed more than love in his life, especially since the feeling could change so easily.

'I'm sorry,' Georgia said.

Max didn't reply. This wasn't how he wanted tonight to go, far from it. Her confession made him realize just how fragile life was. It had been a week since he'd visited his father, and the ache to see him couldn't be curbed by his anger this time.

Instead he forced himself to focus on his surroundings, then Georgia. Tonight he'd wanted to get her so hot she changed her mind about his proposition. And deep down, he wanted to be her first. He knew she wasn't a virgin, but in a lot of ways she was. She'd never experienced pleasure, which was a crime. A testament to just how selfish his sex could be.

But after their heart to heart…

'Max, we're not here to depress ourselves to death. Let's change the subject, 'kay?'

That was a plan he could get behind. 'We should mingle.'

He finished his drink in one go, ignoring the slight burn in his throat. When she did the same, he couldn't help the chuckle that slipped out.

'What? If it's good enough for a guy—'

He pulled her close then, cutting off her protest. Sliding his hands up her arms, he wondered what she'd do if he kissed those shiny lips. God, she was strength, temptation and distraction wrapped up in his most lurid fantasy. 'Have you ever tasted bourbon?'

'No.' Her pupils dilated and he could feel her tremble.

'Would you like to?'

She licked her lips, making them even shinier. Her hands slid up his torso, and he mentally cursed the layers of clothing he wore. He wanted to feel her skin on skin, tongue on skin, over and over.

She grabbed his tie, pulling him so there was only the tiniest gap between their faces. His mouth parted on a gasp and she inhaled.

'It smells kind of smoky, just like your eyes look right now.'

Max couldn't speak. Blood roared in his ears, drowning out the sounds of the music and conversations around them.

Georgia trailed her tongue the length of his lower lip, and he felt the fiery touch right down to his growing erection. She stepped away then, leaving him panting.

'I like it.'

He had no idea if she was talking about the taste of the drink, or the way she'd licked him. Max didn't care which it was, as long as she did it again.

Picking up her clutch she said, 'Let's mingle.'

He was about to veto that idea and suggest they bail, but then Clarissa broke away from the crowd with Marcello's hand in hers.

'Hello, Max. I didn't expect you to come.'

* * * *

The tension in Max was different to what it had been when he was talking about his father. Hell, it was different to what it had been a second ago, when she'd stroked his lip with her tongue. She'd done it to lighten up the conversation. But also because of an uncontrollable urge to taste his lips. And it had been heaven, which Georgia suspected had more to do with the man than the drink. And Max had been tense with arousal.

But now, face to face with his ex and the man who'd stolen her from him, Max didn't look strained from holding back his arousal, this tension was full of anger not lust. His jaw was tight, his expression eerily void of emotion, and his expressive eyes were hard.

The beauty who had just interrupted them had to be Clarissa. She was more stunning than Georgia had feared. With long black curls, a tall willowy figure and a killer red dress, Georgia felt like one of the seven dwarfs facing off against Snow White.

Max's tone was too casual. 'I've no idea why you would think that, Clarissa. Marcello, good to see you again.'

She tried to keep the surprise off her face as Max shook hands with the man who he no doubt hated. She now understood why he didn't want to face the happy couple alone, especially after

Clarissa's cutting comment about not expecting him to come. He didn't want either of them to see how much they'd hurt him.

'This is Georgia Lewis,' he introduced her, pulling her closer with a possessive hand on her hip.

She smiled politely, even as Marcello's dark, creepy gaze dropped to her breasts. Yeah, they were bigger than his date's, but did that matter when she was the most gorgeous woman in the room? Max stiffened at her side and his hand curled into a fist at her hip. She hid the evidence with her arm.

With her sweetest, cavity-inducing smile, Georgia cleared her throat. 'Clarissa, would you mind teaching your date some manners? It's rude to ogle the breasts of someone you've just met.'

Max relaxed his hand and coughed, trying to hide his laugh. Though the beauty queen's mouth gaped, she tightened her hold on Marcello's hand until her knuckles turned white. When he smiled at her, Georgia could see why Clarissa was attracted to him. He was very handsome and had classic Italian features – probably the charm to go with it too.

Still, something about him made her skin crawl.

'We'll catch up with you later,' Max said.

The lovebirds didn't seem to notice them leaving. Clarissa had leaned close to her date and whispered in his ear. He wrapped his arms around her, but Georgia could see the stiff set of her shoulders.

Max tugged her toward the dance floor and she gave up her peeping Tom act on his ex. He grinned down at her as he pulled her into his arms. Reaching up and wrapping her arms around his neck was too easy, like she'd done it a hundred times before. The amusement in his eyes made it hard not to smile back at him.

'I thought your cutting mouth was reserved for me only.' He led her through a slow dance, swaying her around the others with light, easy steps.

Georgia kept up easily, even though dancing like this wasn't something she was used to. 'No. Everyone and anyone who deserves it.'

His grin got wider and her heart stuttered. He pulled her close again and she didn't fight it, knowing how good it felt pressed against him. With Max, she didn't have to call the shots, or take the lead and wasn't that sexy as hell?

Georgia rested the side of her face against his chest, trying to convince herself it was merely for show, to make her guise as his date more believable. Didn't work, but right now she didn't care. Max responded by holding her closer. With one hand he trailed his fingers up and down her spine, making her shiver.

'Tell me something,' he said after a few minutes.

'Depends,' she replied.

His chest rumbled with a silent laugh, and it seemed to resonate through her, lighting her nerve endings and making her clit throb. God, the touching was a bad idea.

Georgia noticed the thinning crowd and lifted her head to see he'd led her over to the other side of the dance floor. They were as alone as they were going to get and anticipation fought against the unease that slithered down her spine in place of his fingers. She looked at him, and his deep-in-thought expression didn't help ease the trepidation.

'It's personal,' he warned.

Georgia swallowed. They hadn't agreed on this being more than an extension of work and she couldn't blame him for assuming. After all, she'd let him touch her, let him pull her close. She'd even licked his mouth, for fuck's sake. But she hadn't made her mind up on it being anything more. Or was her body deciding for her?

'Relax,' he said, stroking her lower back. 'It's not what you think.'

Georgia straightened up and pulled her arms from his neck. He caught her wrists, his thumbs lazily drawing circles over the veins, sending delicious currents through her. God, no man had touched her like this. No man had turned her on this much. Could Max be the one to give her what she'd never had?

'Easy.' His expression turned serious, but he didn't release the gentle hold he had on her wrists. 'Do you always take the lead with men?'

The question caught her off guard. 'What business is that of yours?'

The corner of his mouth twitched, pissing her off and giving her the strength to pull her arms free. He didn't seem deterred by her anger.

'It's not, but you seem more sure of yourself when you do. I've been thinking.'

She crossed her arms, tucking her clutch under her elbow. 'About whether I like it better on top? I thought we'd been through this, I can't—'

'Maybe that's the problem,' he said, deadpan serious. Her chin dipped. 'You try to take control, thinking it will be easier to get what you want. Have you ever thought of surrendering that with someone? Letting them take the lead.'

Well, yeah. About a minute ago, but she'd been thinking about dancing.

Her face burned and she was right back in the moment in her office when she realized he'd read the email. She darted a glance around, but they weren't in hearing distance of the other guests. Didn't stop the shame burning up her neck. Max came closer and she leaned back. He didn't try to touch her, which was smart. Her anger was simmering right below the surface.

'Georgia, imagine surrendering that control to me. Imagine letting all the worry about everything go until there's nothing left but my mouth and hands on your body. Teasing, nibbling and sucking you all over.'

Before she could stop it, the fantasy formed – but it wasn't like others she'd had. She was on a huge four-poster bed with her wrists bound above her head. Max was on top of her, his mouth hot and teasing against her collarbone as he toyed with her nipples. They pebbled and heat flooded between her legs. She closed her eyes, lost in the faux sensations, until his arms came around her for real.

Her eyes snapped open and she shoved at his chest as panic tightened her throat. Though he loosened his hold, he didn't let go.

'People are watching,' he warned.

Her heart was beating so hard, pumping scorching blood through her veins. The pounding between her legs almost hurt and she squeezed at her thighs to get relief. But this was crazy, she wasn't submissive.

'Max, that's not what I want.' The lie didn't convince either of them, so she tried again. 'I'm not some…some…submissive who will kneel at your feet.'

She'd read enough of those kind of romance novels to know that much. Some of the scenes had turned her on, but the pain… She shivered.

'I'd never want you to, but just now whatever you were imagining turned you on. Georgia your skin flushed; you were panting and swaying so much I had to hold you up.'

She couldn't look into his knowing eyes, instead she focused on his black tie. The pain was a deal-breaker, but other things? Georgia didn't know. The thought of his tie around her wrists while he had her in all of those different ways did turn her on.

'I'm not a submissive,' she said again, her voice hard and firm.

He tilted her chin up until she was forced to meet his eyes. They were soft, unexpectedly kind and full of understanding.

'That's a label, honey. One that gets misused all the time. You're strong, confident and extremely sexy. Giving up control in the bedroom doesn't make you any less of who you are. Different things turn different people on.'

'What do you like in the bedroom?' she asked, desperate to get the subject off her.

Max smiled and she focused on his mouth. She'd never wanted anything as much as she wanted to kiss him then. Her whole body burned with the need to know what it felt like. What being with him would feel like.

'I like control, which is how I know we'll work. All you have to do is let me have it, and I'll make sure you get what you need.'

# Chapter 4

Georgia struggled to focus through the lusty haze as Max guided her around the room, introducing her to the designers and their dates. She wanted more champagne, maybe even a bourbon to calm her nerves.

Her mind kept slipping to all the ways Max would take control of her body – if she let him – which didn't help with the meet and greet. Every time he touched her it became more possessive, or maybe that was all in her head.

Could he be like those dominants she read about? He wasn't flashy, didn't have billions in the bank – but the chain of stores was well on its way. Since he moved to New York after successfully launching the Briggs in LA, his forward-thinking had meant the accounts were looking better every year.

And he'd managed to get her here tonight, even though she hadn't wanted to come.

Plus he'd told her he wanted to control her in the bedroom, turning her on more than she thought possible.

'Everything okay?' he asked, low enough for only her to hear.

They were now speaking with a woman she thought was called Melissa, who was pretty, in an understated way. Max had said she designed their Foxy underwear line – which Georgia was wearing at that very moment.

She nodded, not trusting her voice to tell the lie.

Max frowned, then turned back to Melissa and her man. 'Will you excuse us?'

They said their goodbyes and Max led Georgia in the direction of the exit. They'd been at the party for a few hours and she was more than ready to get out of there. Shey and Eloisa were hitting the town tonight and wouldn't be back for hours, but she needed her friends. Max might think it was fine for her to be some kind of submissive, but she didn't and she needed to confer with her besties.

'Are we leaving?' she asked hopefully.

He nodded, but his attention was snagged by Marcello, who had stepped out of the crowd in front of them.

'Leaving already, Briggs?' he asked.

Max tugged her closer, his posture changing so subtly she doubted the man would notice, but Georgia could feel his muscles tighten across his back.

He surprised her again by clapping Marcello on the shoulders, with a smile on his face that didn't reach his eyes. 'Party's almost over.'

Marcello ignored him, his attention flickered to Georgia with that smile that lit up his whole face. 'Pity, I hoped to have at least one dance with you.'

Max stiffened beside her, but before he could lose his cool Georgia used her best weapon against creeps like him. 'Marcello, even if you didn't make my skin crawl, I wouldn't let your tiny hands near me for all the money in the world.'

His smile vanished. 'You're only saying that because you haven't had the chance to be with a real man.'

The dig against Max pissed her off. And him too, if his scowl was anything to go by. Without thinking, she stuck the final knife in. 'I just feel bad for Clarissa. After having Max, then being stuck with what little you're packing, she must be kicking herself. Where is she by the way?'

Marcello's scowl turned deadly and Max pulled her back.

'Watch yourself, Marcello.'

The warning in Max's voice was delivered in a similarly cutting way. The other man stepped back with a strained smile. Max led her into the hotel's lobby. Her heels clicked on the marble floor along with the staccato slap of his loafers.

She tried to gauge his mood, but his expression was unreadable. Shit, had she taken it too far? As well as making her skin crawl, the fact that Marcello had the gall to flirt with her in front of Max had made her want to hit him where it hurts. But she shouldn't have brought Clarissa into it. Her stomach flipped at the idea she'd hurt Max, but for some reason it was the idea that he wanted his ex back that was crushing her insides more.

The cool air hit her face like a slap the second Max opened the door for her. He released her waist, then took hold of her hand. Instead of taking her to the front of the building where the limo would pick them up, he pulled her along the sidewalk.

'Where are we going?' The streets were empty and being smack bang in the middle of the Upper East Side, she didn't worry much about getting mugged.

But she was worried when he tugged her into the shadows at the side of the hotel. 'Max…' She tried to pull her hand free, but he only tightened his hold.

Digging her heels into the concrete, she almost snapped one of the spiky stilettos. 'What the hell are you doing?'

He turned on her then, and the dim light showed his expression. He wasn't pissed off like she expected, but his jaw was tight and his eyes smoldered. A flash fire burned beneath her skin and her heart beat so loud it drowned out the sound of her staggered breathing.

Max lifted her and pulled her legs around his waist. She dropped her clutch as she gripped his shoulders to keep from falling. His mouth attacked hers before she could take another breath. The fiery contact was all it took for her to forget why this was a bad idea.

Her lips parted, allowing him entry, and Max took charge. He tasted smoky and delicious, better than anything she could have imagined. Better than he had earlier. His kiss was born of desperation and she was right there with him. Threading her fingers through the silky waves of his hair, she squeezed her thighs around him tighter, pressed her aching breasts against his chest, and sucked on his tongue like she wanted to suck on his cock.

A deep growl vibrated in his throat, then cool stone met her back. She didn't give a shit that he had her pressed tightly against the wall, didn't care that the chiffon would probably tear as he ground his erection into her.

The bundle of nerves between her legs was just out of reach, and she tried to shift her hips to get some friction, but she couldn't move. She broke away from his mouth, gasping in a lung full of air.

'Max, I need—'

He unwrapped her legs from his waist and placed her back on her feet. Georgia was about to protest when he said, 'I know exactly what you need.'

Before she could register what he was doing, he had her panties at her ankles and was kneeling on the ground in front of her. 'Lift your feet, one at a time.'

She did and he removed the black lace, pausing long enough to tuck her panties into his inside pocket. He pushed her dress up her hips, then lifted her right leg over his shoulder, exposing her to him in the most intimate way. Instead of embarrassing her, her core throbbed and more moisture flooded her pussy.

'Hold onto the pipe. You're going to need the support.'

She tried to move her leg away, but then his thumbs were parting her folds. His breath brushed her clit, making it swell and burn. All she could do not to fall was obey him. She reached both hands up to grab onto the cold pipe.

His forefinger circled her clit and she bucked her hips to get more friction.

'Your cream's everywhere, Georgia. I need to taste it.'

Max dipped his head and then she couldn't protest if she wanted to. His tongue was gentle, teasing, but it sent a shiver through her. She clutched the pipe tighter, trapped in the pleasure coursing through the lower half of her body.

He pressed her hips to the wall until her ass was flattened against the cool brick. Max continued to torture her with his tongue, only sweeping her clit lightly then moving down to her entrance. When he pierced her she was glad she had something to hold onto, because the burn in her lower belly got more intense, like he'd found the G-spot she thought she didn't have and was licking it mercilessly.

Pressure built and built until it got hard to breathe. Unable to move her hips, she thrashed her head from side to side. Little desperate sounds escaped her mouth, but she didn't care as long as he kept doing what he was doing.

Her muscles tightened and his tongue continued to spear into her for a beat, then he stopped. Gasping, Georgia glared at him. Even in the dim light she could see his chin shine with her juices, and it was so hot it stifled her irritation.

'You need to relax. We're not leaving this alley until you come for me, Georgia.'

She squeezed her eyes shut as what she was doing registered. She wouldn't come; she never could. Then he'd never look at her the same way again, knowing she was a freak.

'I can't,' she whispered.

He was quiet for so long, if it wasn't for the fact that his breath still brushed her soaked flesh and her leg was supported by his shoulder, she'd swear he'd left. Metaphorically pulling on her big-girl panties, she opened her eyes to face him.

Which is what he seemed to be waiting for, because he leaned forward and very deliberately sucked her clit into his mouth, his gaze never leaving hers. The bundle of nerves sent jolts through her body – burning jolts that added to the pressure inside. She whimpered and dug her heel into his back to pull him closer. But he released her and she let out a frustrated groan.

'Your body works just fine. Relax. Let me make you feel good.'

'I don't know how.'

He stroked the leg she was using to keep herself up, all the way down to her ankle. His touch scorched through her, even though the chilly breeze brushed her skin.

'Put this over my other shoulder,' he commanded.

She hesitated, not wanting to burden him with her weight. He was built and impossibly huge between her legs, but the conversation she'd been worrying about for hours came back. If he was right, doing this would be like surrendering everything to him. She had to trust him to hold her up, to give her what she needed and the thought didn't only terrify her, it kicked up the inferno burning through her.

*Screw it.*

Georgia lifted her leg and hooked her knee over his shoulder, keeping a firm hold of the pipe. She was fully open to him now, seeing nothing except the top of his head. This position made it hard to tense the lower half of her body, since her focus was split holding on to the cold metal and what he was doing between her legs.

'Honey, I'm going to make sure you enjoy this. I promise.'

Her heart thumped unsteadily at the endearment, but she didn't have time to consider it. The flat of his tongue pressed down on her clit at the same time he slid two fingers inside. Everything doubled. From the fiery burn to the sizzling jolts coming from where he worked her clit.

Her stomach muscles tightened at the need to move, but she was trapped as the joint tortures made her more and more breathless. The pressure built again – so fast it made her head spin – until something felt like it was about to explode. Tears burned her eyes as she knew she was stuck in this agony, having never been able to get past it.

Max must have known. He sucked on her clit so hard she had

to choke back a scream. His tongue flicked the nub faster and his fingers pumped harder. Everything shattered, sending waves of ecstasy through her. It was too much, but not enough. The ripples of pleasure were more extreme than she'd ever thought possible and the rush of emotions that came with it knocked her sideways. So *this* is what she'd been missing out on.

Her whole body twitched as she was moved away from the wall. She couldn't see, or maybe she'd closed her eyes. A minute later her face was pressed against warm silk that smelled delicious, like only Max could, and she was secured to his chest, wrapped in his arms. Her heartbeat pounded in her ears and breathing was so hard she wished it wasn't necessary.

'You're so beautiful when you come. So fucking beautiful.' Max's breath brushed her ear as he spoke, his hands rubbing up and down her spine.

Her heart cracked at the words. She opened her eyes to see him staring at her with what looked like wonder. Surely she should be thrilled to find out she wasn't a freak with a body that didn't work right? Instead the fissure in her heart ached.

This was supposed to be pretend, yet she'd never experienced anything that felt this real.

* * * *

Something that felt suspiciously like pride swelled Max's chest until drawing air into his lungs became a struggle. Christ, this woman in his arms was going to be the end of him. He'd wanted to be the first to give her an orgasm and had succeeded. But that's not why he was so choked with emotion; he was in danger of being a sissy.

Georgia had surrendered her body to him, trusted him completely to know what she needed and he'd given it to her. Her cry when she came, the intensity in which she trembled, and the way she clung to him now fought against his rational self until all he could think was *mine.*

The certainty of it put frost on his libido. Georgia wasn't his; she couldn't be. He was done with relationships, done with being screwed over and rejected and it wouldn't be fair to lead her on by pretending this could be any more than a bit of fun.

But he did still need Georgia on side, especially if he was going to have his revenge on Marcello.

Getting away from her now would be a smart move – just not that easy when she was looking at him like she'd never seen him before. And hell, he knew exactly how she felt. He couldn't take his eyes off her.

'I didn't believe you,' she said.

'I know.'

The chill of the concrete digging into his knees reminded him where they were. He stood, bringing Georgia with him and keeping a hold of her waist when she wobbled.

She laughed a little and it was the loveliest sound he'd ever heard. 'I can't feel my legs.'

Max grinned at her. 'Lesson one; never underestimate me.'

Georgia bent to pick up her clutch. 'Duly noted.'

He took her hand and led her back to the street. People were filtering out now and some primitive part of him didn't want any of them to witness the afterglow of her first orgasm. That was his right, even though the thought was insane. Still, after sending a quick text to his driver he guided her away from the hotel.

'Are you going to tell me where we're going this time?' she asked, but didn't try to stop him.

That made him grin like an idiot, or maybe it was the fact they'd got through a whole night together without arguing. Much. 'To the limo,' he answered.

After a few blocks he spotted the car parked in front of a closed store. Street lights made it easier to see, but he kept scanning the darkness just in case. It was New York they were in, after all.

He opened the door for her then followed her in, desperately trying to keep his eyes off her ass. Having sex now was too risky when his inner caveman was beating the urge to claim her. Georgia shuffled closer and he couldn't resist tucking her under his arm. She was tough though vulnerable; firm yet soft and about a hundred other contradictions he couldn't get his head around.

One thing was sure, when she'd cut Marcello down with a few sentences she'd turned him on so much that in his still-jealous haze he couldn't think of anything other than getting her alone and thanking her the only way he knew how.

'Is this the part where you give me back my panties?' she whispered.

Max reached for the control that would raise the privacy screen, then stopped. With no one watching, there was every chance he'd strip her naked and take her right now. Bad idea. His emotions were running too high and he could tell from the way she looked at him that he wasn't the only one.

'They're mine. I earned them.' He turned to her, making sure his expression was serious.

She glared for a second, then a huge smile stretched her lips. In the overhead light she took his breath away. He'd never seen her smile like that, and his inner caveman roared at him to claim her as his in every way.

'Put that screen up, Max. We're not done.'

Her hand reached for his zipper but he caught her wrist. Her smile disappeared and pain clouded her eyes before she turned her head. Shit.

'We're not done, honey. Just getting started, I promise. But not tonight, okay?'

She looked at him with the fire back in her eyes. 'What's wrong with tonight?'

He loosened his tie, hoping that would make the suffocating feeling disappear. It wasn't her, it was him. If he let them get close now, things could get messy with the turmoil of emotions inside him. But he couldn't tell her that.

'It's getting late and I wanted to check on my father before I go home. I didn't think tonight would work out the way it did.'

Her expression softened with something that looked suspiciously like pity. Max squeezed his eyes shut. Since his conversation with Georgia earlier, Max had wanted to visit. His father's new live-in nurse had called yesterday, saying he was eating less and less. Giving up on life and himself. Why the hell his father still wanted to control these functions, when it seemed he had nothing he wanted to live for – Max included – was a mystery.

'You love him, but you're angry too,' she said.

His eyes snapped open. 'You don't know what you're talking about.' Her wince made him lighten his tone. 'I'm not angry at him, not anymore.'

Georgia's frown was thoughtful. 'Why were you?'

Max gritted his teeth. He didn't want to go there with her, not now. Not ever. And if he could completely crush the anger and resentment toward the old man he would have long ago. She cupped his face in her hands and seemed to stare into his soul. It unnerved him, but also made him want to ask her to come with him. She'd lived through the loss of the last of her family. When his mother died, he'd tried to console his father, never having much time to face his grief. This time it was different – he was watching it happen and didn't know how to stop it.

'You don't have to tell me, but sometimes it helps to talk.' Her thumbs rubbed the hollow of his cheeks and his eyes slid shut.

His anger dissolved slightly as his body relaxed under her touch. The car pulled to a stop too soon, and the warmth of her skin left his.

'Thank you, Max. Tonight was amazing.'

The smile she gave him wasn't a happy one and it tugged at him. He reached for her face before she left, pressing his lips against hers. It wasn't filled with lust, instead gratitude, for everything she'd given him tonight.

But there would be no more heart-to-hearts here. He had to take this back to what it was supposed to be. Pulling his head back, he forced a teasing smile, 'I want you to practice making yourself come this weekend. When I see you on Monday I want you to show me.'

'I think I might need your tongue for that.'

His thumbs skimmed the side of her throat, down to her collar-bone. 'No, you only need to think about me telling you how to pleasure yourself.'

She shuddered. 'I think I can manage that.'

Blood pulsed back into his groin, which was his cue to say goodbye now. He couldn't resist one last kiss, cupping her breasts and tweaking the hard tips with his fingers. She gasped into his mouth, revving him up further. The urge to throw her down and sink into her creamy channel, to claim her, rose up to the surface so fast he had to release her.

'Don't forget your breasts.' His voice was so thick he had to clear his throat. 'I want you to tease your nipples into hard points when you make yourself come.'

Georgia swallowed, then nodded. Her pale skin was flushed and she was breathing hard when she left the limo. Max had to fist his hands on his lap to keep from reaching for her again. Somehow she'd burrowed under his skin, but he was positive time apart would lessen her hold on him. It had to.

# Chapter 5

Anticipation turned Georgia's stomach into knots on Monday morning. Forcing herself to concentrate on work was harder than it should have been. By the time noon came it was as if a raincloud had settled over her, dimming any hope she had of Max contacting her.

She'd done as he asked this weekend, surrendering to his imagined demands over and over again by herself, but the orgasms she'd had didn't even get close to the one he'd given her.

The last two days had been a special kind of torment, so she wasn't really surprised Monday morning wasn't going as she'd hoped. First, there was the burning need to see Max that hadn't vanished and she was beginning to suspect she was developing more than lust for her boss.

But that didn't compare to the lectures from both Shey and Eloisa. They'd made her feel like a silly kid, explaining that good sex – even great sex – wasn't love. How intense pleasure could blur the lines. She'd found that out herself after her first-ever orgasm, but it hadn't been love she'd experienced then; only emotion, and emotion she could deal with.

This waiting for him to contact her – that's what was driving her nuts.

A red light on her desk phone flashed on, indicating a new

voicemail. Georgia frowned at it. It hadn't chimed, which meant someone had dialed straight to the machine.

She picked up the receiver and fetched the message.

*'I hope you studied hard. Your test is in fifteen minutes. My office.'*

Her heart raced as she listened to his voice, deep and husky over the line. Adrenaline pulsed through her veins and her whole body tingled. Oh, he knew how to make a girl want him. But she wasn't going to let him win so easily.

After all, he may take control in the bedroom. Might even boss her around more at work, but she wasn't a pushover, and irritation sizzled right alongside the want. He left the message so she couldn't tell him no.

Just then Janice poked her head into the room, her purple curls bouncing around her face. 'I'm going to the café across the street. Do you want me to bring you something back?'

The part of her that needed to keep her pride got an idea. 'How about I come with you and we can have lunch out?'

'Sure.'

'Great. I need to make a call but I'll be there in a sec.'

Janice left and Georgia dialed Max's voicemail. After his greeting she left a message.

*'We'll have to reschedule. I have a lunch date.'*

Kind of. Technically Janice counted as a date, which was why her voice remained steady. She picked up her handbag and headed out of the room. Janice met her in the corridor.

'Should I ask?' Janice said as they made their way to the store front.

Georgia strove for an innocent expression. 'No idea what you're talking about.'

'Yeah, right, that smirk you're sporting means trouble, if I know you.'

She laughed, feeling lighter than she had all morning. Janice was half right. She would probably end up in trouble. But it was Max's turn to sweat for a while. Payback for the morning from hell.

They made it to the glass entrance of Briggs when one of the security staff stepped in their way. Georgia frowned at him, but she had a sinking feeling she knew what this was about. He couldn't stop her from leaving – it was her lunch hour, for cripes sakes.

'Miss Lewis, Mr. Briggs wants you in his office immediately.'

Ignoring the wide-eyed look Janice aimed at her, Georgia fought to control the anger bubbling below the surface. Did Max want all his staff to find out what they were doing? He couldn't make it more obvious than if he'd put a message out over the store speakers asking for her to go spread her legs wide on his desk.

Though she wanted to tell the man he could let Mr. Briggs know not to hold his breath, she could sense the stares of the gossip girls boring into her. They didn't need a reaction from her to blow the stories out of proportion.

Georgia turned to Janice with what she hoped was an easy smile. 'I'm sorry. Will you bring me back a bagel?'

Janice twisted her lips, like she did when she was trying to work something out. But one good thing about her mentor was that she knew when to keep her thoughts to herself.

'Sure, Georgia. I'll see you after lunch.' Janice skirted around the security guy.

'I'll go right up,' she said with the sweetest tone she could muster.

All the way she seethed, cussing Max out over and over again. The lobby to his office was empty, so Lucy must be on lunch. Well, if he thought he was getting any after this he had another thing coming.

Georgia opened his door without knocking, organizing all the insults running through her mind to find the perfect one to use first.

The words died on her tongue. There were no lights anywhere except for the glow of a small lamp and dozens of candles. His desk was clear and the small conference table he used for meetings was covered with several dishes from the sandwich place across the street.

Max was in his chair wearing a scowl. Pity he'd gone and done all this, because there was no way she could call him out now. She wasn't an ungrateful bitch.

'Close the door,' he instructed, his voice giving nothing away.

Her heart raced as she did what he asked. She leaned against the oak, wondering what the hell she should do. There was no way she was going to let him seduce her, not now all the staff knew where she was spending her lunch hour. And yeah, they might assume she was in trouble for something, but that would change if she didn't get her ass back to her desk pronto.

'I'd no idea you'd planned all this.' She swept her hand around the room to indicate the candles. 'After not hearing from you for most of the day I thought you'd changed your mind.'

'Who's your date with?' he demanded.

She gritted her teeth. He was making it hard for her to keep her cool with his how-dare-you tone. 'Janice. What made you think getting security to stop me from leaving on *my lunch hour* was a good idea? Are you insane? Now everyone will be gossiping about us.'

He smiled then, the tension gone. 'Relax, honey. It doesn't matter what they say. You and I know what's happening here and that's all that matters.'

There it was again, the endearment. Georgia wondered if he called all his lovers by that name and it didn't help much with her pissed levels. 'So you're quite happy for everyone to know you're fucking one of the accounts women?'

He rose, then rounded the desk. She grabbed the door handle, getting ready to bolt. The steel in his blue eyes was loud and clear, even in the dim light. She was thrown back to the week before when she'd been in this very office calling him out while fantasizing about hot, angry sex on his desk.

The lick of arousal in her stomach froze her to the spot. If she gave in now, what would be left of her pride? She had so little since he read the email… No, she had to get out of here, regroup and figure out what to do about Max. Doing anything in the office was a headliner of a bad idea.

Georgia pulled the door open a crack but he was fast. He pushed above the knob and it slammed shut.

She opened her mouth to give him hell but he clapped his hand over her lips.

'No, I don't want the staff to think we're fucking. If anything, I'd prefer they assumed we were in a relationship.'

Her heard swelled with hope, but it was short-lived. She slapped his hand away. 'We're not though. It's some sick, twisted game to get Clarissa back, isn't it?'

If Georgia thought he'd been mad last week, he was absolutely furious now. How could blue eyes look that hard? How could a beautiful face like his twist into something so ferocious? She swallowed and the blood drained from her face, leaving her skin cool and clammy.

That had been the wrong thing to say. It was times like this when she wished she'd been born without a voice box, or maybe some control over what came out of her mouth.

'If you think I'd use you to get back with a woman who publicly humiliated me, you might as well walk out that door right now.' His voice was controlled despite the chill, and it didn't help her anxiety levels.

She was tempted to leave, but then he'd think that's what she really thought. It wasn't, not anymore. She'd had her suspicions about why he needed her by his side. If nothing else, Friday night proved he could handle being in Clarissa's company without Georgia on his arm – or anyone else.

'Then I don't get why we're pretending to be something we're not.'

Max spun her until her body was wedged between him and the door. His erection was thick and hard against her stomach and she couldn't stop the gasp that escaped her lips. The heat that flared between her thighs.

Hell, who was she kidding? She wanted him bad. And she didn't want it all one-sided either. She wanted to make him feel like he'd made her feel on Friday night. She wanted to taste his come, feel all that hard flesh in her palms and mouth. Him surrendering to *her* this time.

'There's nothing pretend about this,' he said, then his lips caught hers.

Georgia tried to stay unaffected, keep a shred of control so she could do what she wanted. The second his fingers tangled in her hair and he tilted her head to get a better angle, her lust levels went off the charts. Struggling to breathe through her nose, she could only take what he gave her. His tongue was thick and full in her mouth, stroking and demanding.

The kiss was too much, though she could sense it was one-sided. She'd pissed him off and the thought he was doing this to get her where he wanted her stung. To keep her sweet so she'd keep up the charade. It was about gratitude to him, not about give and take. Pain wasn't something she could handle and was grateful when the emotion morphed into something hotter, something that pissed her off.

She pushed at his shoulders hard, until he staggered back a step. Taking a firm hold of his tie she used it to pull him around until their positions switched. Though his eyes widened he didn't fight her.

She unzipped his fly, determined to show him they were equals. Make him admit that whatever was between them wasn't just about him giving her pleasure. Her mind fogged with lust as she dropped to her knees on the lush carpet and freed him from his boxers.

There wasn't time to undo the belt or buttons. She wanted to prove to him she wasn't his to do with as he pleased, that she could give right back and he could trust her to. This was her chance to get in the driver's seat and call the shots.

As suspected, his cock was stiff and heavy in her hand, though she didn't spend time admiring the view. She sucked him all the way into her throat, just past comfortable, and groaned. Max's fingers wove into her hair again and she didn't know if it was the head of his length pushing at her gag reflex or the way he tugged her hair that made her eyes water.

Swallowing, she heard him hiss but refused to meet his eyes. She was on a mission to bring him to his knees – like he'd done to her in the alley. Sucking as hard as she could, Georgia used her tongue, lips and throat to work him hard and fast.

'Georgia, *stop!*' His voice was strained, but she heard the undertone of demand.

She was too into this to stop. He needed to know that he was her boss at work, but her life was lived the way she wanted to. As she milked a delicious shot of bittersweet pre-come from him, she also needed this for herself. She wanted to give him this.

Max's hands cupped her head, then gently pushed her back an inch. She fought against him but he was too strong. His dick slipped from her mouth with a wet popping sound. He was breathing hard as he stared down at her with confused lust.

'What…the…hell?' he asked.

'I want to do this. Now.'

Before she could wrap her lips around him again, he hauled her up to her feet. Struggling, she tried to take hold of him in her hand but it was pointless. It wasn't pain that made her blood run cold and diverted her gaze to the floor. Rejection washed through her, wiping away the last of the heat. It couldn't be clearer that they'd never be equals than if he'd spelled it out to her.

Max's heart was beating every ounce of blood he had into his cock, but her now-vulnerable state hurt more than the blow job he hadn't let her finish. He must be losing his goddamn mind, because that was the best he'd ever had – she'd even told him she wanted to do it – and he'd stopped her.

Tilting her face up, he studied her flushed cheeks and wide, embarrassed eyes. He was glad he put an end to it. If she was

feeling half of what he was, her emotions were all over the place. So much for some time off putting distance between them. Instead, it seemed to make them both so frustrated they had an out-of-control sparring match that ended rough and a bit wild.

'Didn't you enjoy it?'

Max tucked himself back into the prison of his slacks. 'Georgia, you have no idea how much I did.'

She stepped away from him, which felt like a blow to his chest. The only saving grace was the fire in her eyes. She wasn't vulnerable anymore. Thank God.

'Then why stop me?' she asked.

'I didn't want this to be about me. I promised you'd get more from us and I'm keeping my word. Five more seconds and you'd have sucked my brains out.'

Her lips twitched up at the corners and she took a step closer. 'That's what I want. I want to give you what you gave me on Friday.'

Max took both her hands in his and used them to pull her flush against him. Looking down to see those puckered lips had a fresh flow of blood pounding south. He shook his head to clear the haze. 'It didn't feel right having you on your knees, especially after our conversation on Friday.'

Her lips parted, but he quickly pinched them together.

'And you're right. I shouldn't have asked you up here to mess around. I never thought about the gossip and I don't want those women to make you feel uncomfortable. If you like, we can pick up where we left off tonight?'

He released his hold on her mouth, but for once Georgia didn't speak straight away. A little frown appeared above her eyebrows and he longed to smooth it away. But he didn't touch her.

She crossed the room to the table, running her finger along the wood. It was like she'd pulled away from him, more than just physically, and everything in him was pushing him to get her back, and he took a step closer. Holy shit, when had a woman had this much of an effect on him?

'Why did you do all this, Max? There's no one here but the two of us. We could have screwed and still had time after to get lunch. Separately.'

Raking a hand through his hair, he blew out a breath. Saying anything now would be too telling. It would lead her on, give her hope they could blossom to more. He was done tearing himself wide open to get left over and over again.

She turned to him, leaned back against the table and folded her arms across her chest – making her breasts press higher. A stronger, more carnal, arousal ripped through him and it took every ounce of willpower he had to take a casual step back to lean against the door. The picture of ease on the outside, even though he was almost vibrating with need for her.

'How about I tell you what I think?' Georgia said with bravado, but her eyes were shadowed with doubt. 'You want me, but you want to compartmentalize everything you're feeling into a certain category – that would be lust, by the way. All this, it's because you wanted to spend time with me. Time not spent fucking.'

He gritted his teeth but didn't say a word. What the hell was there to say that wouldn't make this worse?

After a few seconds the air was so thick with tension he thought he might choke. The serious expression she wore became edged with doubt.

Georgia shook her head. 'You're not going to admit it, are you?'

Max wanted to reach for her then, but that would give her false hope. He doubted he would break her when they ended – she'd been through so much and was stronger than anyone he knew. Still, no way would he take that risk. Not with her.

She studied him for what felt like forever. Finally she crossed his office, stopping a foot away from him. He could reach out, touch her. If her eyes hadn't hardened, he might have.

'I think it's best if we quit whatever this is while we're ahead, don't you?'

The question was most likely rhetorical, but he wanted to

scream *no*.

'I'm leaving now.'

She didn't meet his eyes as he stepped out of the way to let her past. He had to fist his hands against the urge to grab her and never let go. Fear froze his chest until breathing became impossible, but he didn't know if it was her walking away from him or the way she choked him up with so much want and need.

He didn't have time to process. The ringtone he dreaded hearing and could never ignore made the blood drain from his face.

# Chapter 6

*Holy shit.*

She was crying, actually crying. Drops of moisture trailed down both of her cheeks as she crossed the room to the corridor. Pausing, Georgia swiped a finger under each eye and stared up, trying to stop the insanity.

Yeah, she was hurting. Hurting over a guy who didn't want more from her than some strings-free fun. Oh and someone to stand by his side at functions so he could save face in front of his ex. She'd thought – hoped – the effort he'd made for their meeting meant something to him. Had even put her pride on the line, she'd been that sure. Or that hopeful.

For the first time ever, she had no idea what to do. Going back to work and pretending the conversation with Max didn't just happen was a given, but after? Had she just ended things between them before they'd even started? Hell, did she want anything to get started?

Pushing away from the wall, she took a step down the corridor. The sound of his door opening made her turn. Max's face was pale and he was holding the door frame with shaking hands.

A glimmer of hope that this was all for her dispelled the burn in her eyes and made her heart flutter, until she gave herself a mental slap.

If he looked this upset, the man who could hide behind a mask of emotionless composure … 'Has something happened to your father?'

Max swallowed, then ran a shaking hand through his hair. 'He's…'

*Oh God, no.*

'At the hospital. They think he's had a heart attack.' The strain in his voice was evident and his wild eyes made her heart throb.

'You're going to see him?' she asked, knowing it was a stupid question.

Max staggered forward a step. He nodded, pulled his keys out of his pants pocket, but they dropped to the floor. Shit, he couldn't get behind the wheel like this. He'd wind up in the ER right next to his father.

Georgia crossed the space between them and swiped his keys from the floor. 'I'm calling a cab. You can't drive.'

He shook his head and waves of hair fell across his forehead. She wanted to push it back, to touch, to comfort. 'Max, don't be an idiot.'

'There isn't time,' he said. 'Do you have a license?'

She did, but she hadn't been behind the wheel since she'd moved to New York – never mind behind the wheel of a sports car. There were a million other reasons why nodding her head, letting him lead her through the store while she almost jogged to keep up with his long strides, then sliding into the driver's seat was a bad idea.

But it was Max's father, maybe his last chance to see him, and hers. How could she refuse to help?

Max didn't say a word, even when she stalled the huge machine at the first set of lights they came to. Glancing at him, she could see a frown marring his brow and his hands were fists against his thighs. In that second she knew she was right, he was angry at his father. But why?

That question plagued her all the way to the hospital. Not that she had any business worrying about Max's relationship with his father. He'd made it pretty clear he didn't want to talk about it on Friday. Now any hopes of what they could have had been crushed, but she shouldn't be thinking about that now. She pulled up at the entrance.

'I can park up then get a cab back to work,' Georgia offered, but had no idea if he heard her.

His gaze remained fixed on the front of the building, the expressionless mask he wore back in place. She wished she could see his eyes to get an idea of what he was feeling.

'Max?'

Blowing out a breath, he turned to her and her heart sank. Pain and fear were so clear in his eyes that she mindlessly reached out. Cupping his smooth jaw with her hands, she stared at him with all the sympathy and support she wanted to offer.

'Come with me,' he said, covering her hands with his and holding them to his face. He closed his eyes.

Georgia's heart swelled and throbbed. She wanted to, she really couldn't say no, but this time she wasn't in danger of sleeping with him, it was losing her heart to him that scared her. He'd told her he didn't want more, told her exactly what he could offer her and nothing else.

Maybe Clarissa had done such a number on him that his heart was broken beyond repair. Maybe it made him too scared to take the next leap. Georgia had never taken that leap either. She'd thought she'd been in love a few times, but none of those guys had made her feel the way he did, and she didn't even mean the way he made her come.

She slid her hands out from under his. Max's eyes opened and at the shake of her head they grew icy, spearing her again. If she'd thought heartbreak was hard before, what would throwing herself at him feel like when he'd never accept her as more than a temporary fling?

Without another word he left his car. Georgia forced herself to drive to the car park, put the ticket on the window, and lock up. Only then did she realize she had to give him back his keys.

She slipped her cell out of her handbag and dialed Eloisa's direct line. It went straight to voicemail, so she tried Shey's. With every ring her heart raced faster and faster. She wanted to run after Max, to believe giving up the last part of her heart to him wouldn't matter, that she'd get over him when they were over.

But that way led to trouble and she wasn't thinking clearly.

Shey answered as Georgia was about to hang up. 'I'm screwed, Shey. Really fucking screwed.'

* * * *

Everything was white. The walls, the chairs, even the linoleum on the floor. Max stared at a faded footprint next to the door of the waiting room, the faint smell of industrial bleach turning his stomach. Or maybe that was waiting on the news that his father had finally got his wish.

It had nothing to do with the way it felt to have Georgia hold his face, offer him comfort when he'd almost lost it trying to pull himself together. She'd left him when he'd really needed her, and wasn't that the theme song for his life?

More proof the old man was killing himself for a myth. Then again, maybe Max was the only person on the planet who didn't deserve the kind of happiness other couples found.

The door opened and his breath stilled in his lungs. Georgia stepped into the room, an apology clear in her eyes. He couldn't speak, staring seemed to be all he was good for at the moment. Had she changed her mind? His throat got thick with hope.

Until he saw the silver glint in her hands and he sucked in a breath. She'd come to give him back his keys. Max shuttered his expression and rose, towering over her in the creepy room. He took his keys with a dismissive 'thanks', tucked them into his suit trousers then picked up a glossy magazine from the table. He'd no idea what it was as he returned to the seat, but the pictures of celebrities dressed up gave him something to look at that wasn't her.

'My friend Shey will be happy to hear you read her magazine.' Georgia's voice was close and he looked up to see her right in front of him.

Max glanced at the cover. 'Who doesn't love *Glamorous*?'

She smiled, but it didn't reach her eyes. 'Bet it beats staring at these walls. Who thought a white-themed room would be comforting?'

He shrugged, unsure of why she was lingering and making small talk. It was nice, though, distracting. The scent of her Dior perfume filled the air, dimming the clinically clean smell of the room.

'How is he?' she asked, concern pinching her forehead.

He wanted to smooth the lines on her face, anything to avoid thinking about why he was here. 'Stable, I think. I'm waiting for the doctor now.'

Her hands twisted together in front of her. She eyed the chair next to him. 'That seat taken?'

He almost smiled at the clichéd line. 'Depends. If you're staying because of some misplaced guilt, don't bother.'

'Max, I'm here because I want to be here. I said no because it scared me *how much* I want to be here.'

Georgia tugged at the hem of her dress, dropping her eyelids and hiding her emotions. It cracked his restraint, the whole shitty day had. From having her walk out on him at the office when he wanted nothing more than for her to stay, to the phone call and her refusal in the car.

He threw the magazine down on the chair. 'It's taken now.'

Georgia paled, so he quickly pulled her onto his lap. She gasped and dropped her handbag on the floor. 'Max, what are you—'

Her lips were as tempting as they'd always been. Now they were soft, pliant and a shocked 'o' beneath his. Max kept it slow, trying to hold back the fiery arousal he knew would rip through his veins the second things sped up, but slow didn't work. The burn wasn't as urgent now. Instead it smoldered through him until he felt almost boneless.

Georgia's palms cupped his face again as he held her close, kissing her like he'd never kissed her before. Hell, like he'd never kissed anyone before. The kiss was about more than distraction, it was all the things he knew he shouldn't feel or say or promise. For these few seconds, he was going to feel it all.

She broke away first, but didn't make a move to stand or shift from his lap. Instead she wrapped her arms around his neck and pulled him close. Max returned the hug, burying his face in her neck, smelling her perfume and the hint of rose shampoo. Fuck it, he could allow himself this. Allow himself to feel for a little bit longer.

The next time the door cracked open it was to let a doctor with a clipboard enter.

Georgia shifted to sit next to him and took his hand. He thought it might be to offer support, but she was trembling. A glance was all it took to see she cared what happened to his father, which set off a turmoil of other, more powerful, emotions. Anger boiled through him, swift and too powerful to restrain.

'Mr. Briggs, your father's awake. He's asking for you.'

# Chapter 7

Georgia might as well have had a dictionary of medical terms thrown at her head, knocking out everything the guy had said. Max seemed to understand, though. He asked all the right questions at the right places.

All she could make out – the most important part – was that Maxton Briggs was weak but on the mend. They were pumping him full of all the nutrients he'd lost, and though she wondered why he needed so much, she kept the question to herself. Max would have a chance to speak with his father, maybe even make things right between them, and that's what mattered.

The three of them walked down the corridors and her nose wrinkled at the smell of total cleanliness, like someone had thrown up bleach and disinfectant and left it out to dry. She kept hold of Max's hand, offering him comfort, but at the same time keeping the contact she was starting to crave from him.

Shey had done the best-friend job, talked her out of putting her heart on the line for a man who couldn't open his, but one glance at him in the room, looking alone and broken, Georgia threw caution to the wind. This wasn't about her. This was about helping someone she cared about through a tough time. Something she didn't have until she met her besties. No way could she leave Max by himself.

She stopped at the door to the room and tried to pull her hand free. Max held on tighter.

The doctor looked down at their hands, then said 'You can both go in but try not to stay long. He needs rest.'

Keeping her mouth shut was for the best. The doctor didn't need to know they weren't a couple and that Max should go in alone. Not that Max was down with that plan. After a deep breath he opened the door and tugged her in with him.

Georgia tried to keep the shock off her face. The room was full of medical crap, beeping machinery hooked up to Mr. Briggs, and her old boss was surrounded by bags of clear liquid pumping stuff into his veins. He was so much thinner than when she'd last seen him, not even two months ago. Now his skin was gray and his eyes sunken.

Max's grip on her hand tightened when Maxton looked up at his son. Then his gaze flickered to their joined hands, making her wish Max had left her outside. Her old boss smiled.

'Lovely to see you here, Miss Lewis,' Maxton said.

She chanced a glance at Max's face and her eyes blurred. He looked so angry, with his clenched jaw and hard eyes. He glared at his father like he'd committed the worst crime in history.

'Thanks, Mr. Briggs. I drove Max here. You gave us all a bit of a scare.'

He looked at Max then. Really looked at him, and his ancient eyes grew sad.

'Father.' Max nodded, his tone clipped. 'How are you feeling?'

Maxton's eyes shone bright with emotion. The tension between the two men radiated throughout the room and Georgia wanted nothing more than to bolt. This was private time, family time, and she was interrupting.

'I'm sorry, my son. I'm… sorry.' The words were whispered, and Mr. Briggs closed his eyes.

Max's hand clenched hers so tightly it almost bent her bones. At her gasp, he eased off but didn't look at her. His attention was on his father, a splinter of his former self, hooked up to tubes, air and monitors.

Silence dragged until the soft snores of Max's father filled the room. The doctor told them not to stay long, but she figured Max would want to. It was clear Max and his father had to talk. Max hadn't accepted the apology although she'd no idea why someone would have to be forgiven for having a heart attack.

They never settled into the plastic chairs in the room, instead remained standing at the door. She shifted her weight from foot to foot, unsure what to do now. Max turned to look at her with an eerily blank expression. Not even his eyes held any sign of how affected he was.

'We should go,' he said with a dead voice.

Georgia pressed her lips together and nodded. It wasn't her business if he stayed or went. Without releasing her hand, he led her out of the hospital at a slower pace than when they left work.

They were outside when curiosity got the better of her. 'You're going back when you drop me off?'

Every muscle in his body seemed to tense as he led her through the car park. They were at his car and he was opening the door for her to get in before he spoke. 'Not tonight.'

Georgia wanted to say more but he swooped down and kissed her hard. Not like the kiss on his lap in the waiting room, where she'd been warmed down to her bones. This was about their shared fire and passion and lust.

He ended the kiss looking as desperate for air as she was. Emotion had come back into his expression. Emotion and need that mimicked hers.

'Get in the car,' he instructed.

Georgia did as he asked and soon they were speeding through New York, much quicker than she had. Her apartment wasn't on this side of Manhattan, though, and she knew then that this was the next step. It was make-or-break time for them both.

She had to tell him to take her home, didn't she? Any more

kisses like the one at the hospital and she'd be gone for sure. But could she walk away from him now, when it was so obvious he needed her?

Torn, she chewed on her lip and risked a glance at him. What she saw helped her make up her mind.

* * * *

The sane part of Max knew he was out of control. Dragging Georgia away like that and kissing her without shielding his intent wasn't fair to either of them. She was an itch he hadn't been able to scratch for so long. And now she was here, he didn't want anyone else, and he needed the distraction.

Max's logical side screamed to back the fuck up and think about it, because he didn't just need the distraction of sex. But his selfish, irresponsible side convinced him he needed Georgia, with a clarity that drove him to smother that sensible part of himself.

Pulling into his building, he realized he had to give her the choice. She hadn't protested, but he was in a shitty mood and might have scared her.

'We both know what happens if you come up. Is that what you want? The time to say no is now, Georgia. When we get inside there's no going back.'

She was too quiet as he parked up. When he turned to her she was squeezing the seat like it tethered her to the earth. His shitty mood evaporated and an ache formed in his chest.

In a calmer tone, he said, 'I want you, I want this, but I'll understand if you don't. I won't hurt you or make you do anything you don't want to. You don't have to be afraid of me.'

Her grip relaxed on the leather. 'I'm not scared of you. I know you won't force me to do anything I don't want to do.'

The band across his chest loosened. 'Do you want to come up?'

Georgia turned to him with one of her eyebrows raised. 'That's like asking if I want a new pair of shoes.'

'Duh?' At her nod, Max smiled for the first time since she'd walked out of his office.

They were both out of the car and heading for the elevator as fast as they could go with Georgia's crazy-high heels. The lilac shift dress she wore complemented her honey-blonde hair, which he couldn't wait to free from the intricate twist at the back of her head.

The second the metal doors closed he set about doing just that, tugging her close and kissing her with all the need and desperation pounding through him. A few pins dropped to the floor, then all those silky waves spilled over his hands. His cock was hard, leaking at the tip, and grinding into her stomach. With every moan, with every gasp from her the sensations racked up until he was bursting with the primal need to take her. Claim her.

He kicked the door of his apartment closed while breaking as little contact as possible from the tangle of limbs she had him in. Her hands fumbled with his belt for a second before giving up and unleashing him through his zip instead. She gripped his dick, drawing a strangled moan from his throat.

'Too… close… we need to… slow—'

She cut him off by dropping to her knees on his thick carpet and taking him. The second he was back in that warm silky mouth Max slumped back against the wall, cracking his head off the corner of a painting before it fell to the floor. He didn't give a shit if the glass smashed.

He wanted to look down, but couldn't find the energy to open his eyes. She was pulling him deep into her mouth, swallowing around the head, while her fisted hand worked him hard. His thigh muscles tensed as he felt the first spark at the bottom of his spine, the only warning he got.

'Georgia, I'm going to—'

She sucked him harder and deeper, totally without mercy. The orgasm slammed into him from behind and shot out of him in a dizzying flash. His head cracked off the wall again as he cursed, the pleasure going and going, building and contracting through him while her tongue and palms soothed him through the spasms.

It took him a minute to open his eyes when she let go. Georgia stood now, a half-smile tilting her swollen lips. Max pulled her close, kissing her thoroughly with his tongue and tasting himself along with her. It was so hot his heart got moving again, pounding sizzling blood through his veins.

This time it would be about her. This time he'd give Georgia all her firsts before he allowed himself to be satisfied. Max lifted her, carried her through to the sofa and sat her on the edge at the back.

'I hear sofa sex is *hot*,' she said with a smile.

'It can be. Now I want you to show me how you did with your homework.'

Her skin flushed a shade darker, especially as he slid up her dress to reach the string supports of her panties. Max grinned. 'Thong?'

She nodded and a fresh pulse of heat travelled south.

'Do I ever get the other ones back?'

'Depends.' He tugged her panties to her knees and let them fall down her calves to land on the floor.

'On?' she pressed.

'How well you do. Now lie back.'

Her brows furrowed and he took her hands so she didn't go too fast. Though her eyes shadowed with doubt as she exposed herself to him, she lay back until her head rested on the seat of the sofa. He propped some pillows under her shoulders, ignoring the feel of his semi-hard cock against her thigh.

The upside down position meant her dress ruffled just below her ribs and when he rose it took him a second to pull himself together. On Friday it had been too dark to get a good look, despite the up-close-and-personal approach he'd used. But with her legs open and spread, her toned stomach bared and her hair fanning out over the pillow, she took his breath away.

'Fuck.'

Max drew the tip of his finger across her parted folds. They glistened with her arousal and his head throbbed with the need to take her now. He was almost on his way to solid, it would be easy to slide himself in and he'd be hard again in seconds.

But he had other plans.

Pushing her knees wider, he dipped his head to get a closer look. 'Make yourself come for me.'

# Chapter 8

Something inside Georgia was broken, or maybe not. Her whole body trembled with the adrenaline fizzling through her veins while her heart cantered faster than ever. She'd never been this exposed to anyone, had never masturbated in front of a lover, and the thrill of fear gave her the courage to do it.

With a shaking hand, she slid her palm across her bared stomach. Max's gaze was fixed on her pussy with eyes darker than she'd ever seen on him. His jaw strained and his hands on her knees gripped her harder as she reached her mound. Thank God she'd kept up her bikini wax!

Her flesh was warm and slick with her juices, so much so he would be able to see it. Being on her knees, having all his stiff flesh in her mouth and throat had done that. Max didn't just turn her on or get her body revved up. That was too easy for a guy like him. He pushed the boundaries of what she'd thought was safe and controlled, and look what going along with him had done on Friday night! For once she didn't want to question or protest. She wanted to surrender. Everything.

She'd worry about the consequences later.

Georgia sought out her clit and started rubbing hard and fast. It hurt a bit, though her touch and his gaze caused more than tingles in the pit of her stomach.

'Slow,' he commanded. 'At first anyway.'

Getting into the sensations, Georgia ignored him. She closed her eyes, her head lolled from side to side on the cushion with each stroke, and she had to gasp for air. Blood pooled in her head, making the sensations more intense. Now she understood the weird position he'd put her in.

The pressure built in an almost painful twist in her stomach, the epicenter building in her clit was almost too much to bear but she knew what came next. Bliss. Pure pulsating bliss, and nothing in the world could stop her getting there.

The pressure disappeared at the same time she realized her arm was gripped to the side of her hip in Max's hand. Her eyes flew open and she couldn't help but scowl at him as her body jerked from the lack of touch.

He grinned at her and shook his head. 'I said *slow*. It isn't a race.'

Her strangled reply was meant to be an insult, but even she couldn't make out the words.

After planting a kiss on her throbbing flesh, Max licked his lips. 'You taste so fucking sweet. It's addictive.'

*Thank God.* That meant more of his tongue. Down *there.* The pulsing nub swelled as if trying to reach his lips, but he lifted his head away from her. 'Max!'

His smile strained. 'I'm solid for you Georgia, have been since your fingers found your clit. I want to fuck you right now, over this sofa, hard and fast.'

His words took her to a new level of turned on. It wasn't just blood sizzling her veins, it was need. She wanted every inch of him inside her, doing exactly what he said. Pushing herself up, she was about to agree when he slid two fingers inside of her.

Max groaned deep in his throat. 'Fuck, you're so smooth and hot. Well,' His fingers brushed over that spot that made her whole pelvis burn and she flopped back onto the cushions. 'except for this part. My favorite part.'

'Max.' Georgia's breath tore through her lungs, in and out, but it didn't stop her from feeling dizzy.

He didn't ease up, sweeping slow strokes over and over her G-spot until the pressure built and built. Achy, desperate, she reached for her clit to speed things up, but he batted her hand away.

'I want to make you come like this,' he said.

Her patience expired. 'Do it then!'

His throaty chuckle only riled her, and that wasn't a good thing to be when he had her on the edge of heaven. At least he increased the tempo of his fingers, pumping so hard and fast the pressure built into a sweet pain she now recognized. Relaxing the muscles in her pelvis, she let the dam burst. Shudders and spasms claimed her breath, her heart beat, her sense of time passing.

Not that he gave her any. Max whipped off his shirt and his pants were next. She really tried to pull her dress over her shoulders, but it only got as far as her bra. Plus his carved body on full display was too much of a distraction.

He lifted her until she was perched on the back of the sofa again with his jaw so tight she thought he might crack his molars. A glance down told her it wasn't because she weighed too much, and his muscles weren't just for show. Nope, his cock was hard and a little shiny at the tip.

He grabbed the bottom of her dress and he whipped it over her head. For a second he just stared at her half naked body in wonder.

'We need…' He looked around, as if his lounge would give him answers. 'Shit.'

'What's wrong?' she asked.

Max stepped back and scrubbed a hand through his hair. Her skin goosed at his withdrawal. Especially since she saw how hard he was. How much he wanted this.

'I don't have protection.'

*Oh.*

Georgia swallowed, unable to understand the floaty warmth filling her chest. Somehow knowing he didn't have a ready supply to hand for a number of woman guests made the corner of her lips tilt up. Thankfully she had a solution to their little problem.

'I'm—'

Anastasia's *I'm Outta Love* chimed from her handbag and she sighed. She could ignore Eloisa and hope she went away. Pity her friend was persistent. She probably had one of those stalking apps hidden on her iPhone.

'I'm going to switch it off. I'll just be a minute.' Georgia eased off the sofa and headed for the hall where she'd ditched her handbag.

It didn't take long to find and, aware of her nakedness, she bolted back to the sofa but froze as soon as she saw him. He'd pulled on his suit trousers and was in the process of buttoning up his shirt.

'What's going on?' She put her bag down on the coffee table and covered her tingly bits.

'I should probably take you home.' He didn't look at her, just scooped her thong and dress up off the floor. 'There are all kinds of crazy shit going through my head now, and after our conversation today it's probably best we don't take this further.'

There it was again, the traitor sting in her eyes. She *would not* cry over him again. That he had this much power over her, that she had been stupid enough to think she could still do this with him and deal with the consequences, made her mad.

Grabbing her clothes, she pulled the dress over her head then stuffed the thong in her bag.

'You know what this is? Fear. You're a fucking coward, Max.' She picked up her bag, ignoring the widening of his eyes. 'You're angry at the world since Clarissa left you, and now that your father's sick you're blaming him for something he can't control. I can believe your head's a mess. I wish you'd let me in so I could help, but you're too scared. I was right today, wasn't I? You do give a shit about me. Why else would you be sending me away now?'

Her phone started booming out Christina's *Can't Hold Us Down*, but she didn't want to speak to Shey either.

Max was quiet for a second, probably waiting for her to answer the call. When she made no move to reach for her cell, he said,

'What does it matter, you're leaving.'

*What the…?* 'You told me to!'

Her heart was beating too fast again, her breath coming in pants and she ground her teeth. Hadn't he just insisted he was taking her home? The guy was a total head fuck/heart breaker. Or was there something she was missing?

Max had retreated to the sofa and faced the fireplace. A flare of heat licked her pelvis at the memory of being there minutes before, which now felt like days. He was pushing her away, probably had been from the first night he took her out. She realized then she knew nothing about him. Friday night he'd furrowed out the necessary information about her, what he assumed to be the key to making her come. But other than finding out he didn't want Clarissa back, what did she know?

*Screw it; she had nothing more to lose.*

'Why are you so mad at your father?' she asked.

Max turned to her and the light of the artificial flames danced over the side of his face, making his tan skin and hair golden. 'He's given up.'

'On?' she persisted, suspecting the answer. Dread trickled into her stomach, leaving her cold.

He studied her for so long with those shadowed eyes she didn't think he'd answer. Her insides shifted as her mind played over the scene from the hospital room, the loss of nutrients, weight and Maxton's apology. It all added up to something ugly.

'What do you think?' he asked, but she guessed it was rhetorical. 'All he gives a shit about is that his designers don't walk before…'

*Before he took himself out of the picture.* Georgia crossed the room to him, her heart swelling so much it got hard to breathe.

God, no wonder he was messed up. And she could understand anger. His father had given up on life but not on the person who had screwed Max over? She would be pissed too if the tables were turned.

Sitting next to him, she took his hand and whispered, 'I'm so sorry.'

He ignored her and turned back to look at the ribbon flames dancing in the fireplace, giving the illusion of a warmth she didn't feel.

'You were right, you know,' he said.

She bit her tongue so she didn't cut off his confession. Sighed in relief when he said, 'I am starting to feel more for you than I should.'

He turned to her then and the ice was back in his eyes. 'It wasn't fair to tell you today, probably isn't now, but I can't bullshit you anymore. I appreciated you being at the hospital more than you know, so I owe you the truth.'

With startling clarity, she saw in his expression that nothing had changed, even though he did care about her. Max still wanted a temporary fling, maybe not even that anymore. Cripes, what was she supposed to do with that?

Georgia swallowed against the lump in her throat. 'So you want to stop?'

He nodded. 'I think that's for the best.'

'Right.' Georgia rose slowly, not trusting her thigh muscles to work. 'And the functions?'

He rose too, pulling his keys from his pants. 'I couldn't ask that of you now. Come on, I'll take you home before your friends put out a search party.'

She didn't ask him how he knew it was her friends, though the personalized ringtones might have clued him in. In fact, Georgia didn't have much to say at all as Max led her out of his apartment and down to his car.

All the fighting against him, all the internal struggles and overpowering emotions since he'd asked her to the ball felt pointless now and so not worth the hassle.

* * * *

Shey and Eloisa were on the sofa when she got home. The furniture had been rearranged so there was only the shaggy white rug separating the empty armchair facing the sofa. There was no television on, or laptops or even music. It was times like this Georgia wished she could afford rent on her own Manhattan pad, but with her salary she'd be lucky if she could manage a basement apartment in Brooklyn.

Ditching her bag on the coffee table, she thought through her options. She could walk back out the door, go to the nearest bar and order a bottle or two of tequila; retreat to her bedroom and be alone with her thoughts; or girl-up and get this over with. After all, they'd follow her if she tried to bail.

'What is this?' she asked as she settled into the chair.

Eloisa shared a look with Shey, who nodded, then she turned back to Georgia. 'An intervention.'

Georgia groaned and leaned back in the chair. She should have followed through with the tequila plan.

'Before you butt in, we have something to say,' Shey began.

Georgia glowered at them both.

With all the tact of a prosecutor, Eloisa continued. 'Let's look at the facts. First, you came to us because you didn't want to be his fake girlfriend with benefits. We helped you out, prepared you for a meeting with him that was supposed to put him in his place.'

'Second,' Shey chimed in. 'You ignored our advice, then ended up in an alley with your legs around his neck having your first orgasm. I don't know whether to be impressed by that or mad at you.'

Shey's sly smile brought out Georgia's, despite the fact her friends had her up against a wall and were verbally pelting her with boulders.

'And third,' Eloisa said with that air of authority only a lawyer could pull off. 'You called us for advice today before you went to the hospital and then completely ignored it.'

Her friends looked at her expectantly, like she was supposed to be asking for atonement or some shit. 'They're hardly cardinal sins.'

Eloisa pinched the bridge of her nose, while Shey's amber eyes softened. 'We know. We're just worried about you. You *never* waste this much energy or emotion over a guy.'

Yeah, because there had never been a guy like Max. Not that it mattered now.

Her silence drew Eloisa's scrutiny. 'You're falling for him.'

She shrugged. 'Doesn't matter. He's made it clear it can't go any further.'

'Why?' Shey asked.

Her throat burned as she told them the whole story – leaving nothing out. A few tears were shed, but after the day she'd had there wasn't much she could do about that. By halfway through she was on the sofa in the middle of them both with a glass of much-needed white wine in her hand that they filled up for her over and over.

When she was finished, Shey hugged her. 'I'm so sorry, Georgia.'

Yeah, she was too.

Georgia finished the last of the wine and Shey took the glass through to the kitchen. Her head was fuzzy, but then she'd downed most of the bottle herself in record time.

Eloisa had been silent through her confession, but now she was frowning. 'You need to go after him. He wants you and actually cares about you, so there's something you're missing that's holding him back. Go get what you want. It's the only way you'll ever be happy.'

She spoke so quietly Georgia knew it wasn't something she wanted Shey to hear. When the gorgeous brunette returned with a fresh bottle and a tub of ice-cream, Eloisa bounced off the sofa and headed straight for the DVD collection while she was left reeling at her friend's weird advice.

'We need something funny, with no sappy love story,' Shey said.

Georgia didn't concentrate on the movie. Her mind was too consumed with what it was she was missing.

# Chapter 9

The rest of the week rolled by too fast. Every day Georgia had gone to work wondering if today was the day she'd bump into Max and endure the horrible awkwardness. Or the longing for him would spill out in the form of begging. But his car hadn't been in the car park when she got to Briggs, and wasn't there when she left either.

Come Friday night she wanted to curl up on the sofa with two guys, Ben & Jerry, watching crappy TV into the middle of the night. She never seemed to get what she wanted these days.

She was pounced on the second she got home by two annoying jackasses who made sure she'd slipped into something sexy. Now they were at Club Zero, hours earlier than usual, ordering margaritas instead of shots. The mirrored wall behind the bar showed a different person to the one she felt standing next to her friends. Georgia's hair was tousled and hung loose. Her make-up was smoky, with only light-pink gloss highlighting her lips. The dark-rose dress she wore belonged to Eloisa, so it was more daring than elegant.

'Drink up,' Shey said, pushing a huge glass into her hand. 'Then we hit the tequila. Tonight's going to be *fun*.'

Georgia pulled her lips in a smile and held her glass up. They'd managed to flog better tables since they'd arrived before most of the swarms. Something Shey had probably instigated on purpose to snag Georgia a well-packaged distraction. Eloisa was too quiet, like she didn't agree with the plan.

She was too far gone wallowing in her own self-pity to worry about why Eloisa was keeping secrets from Shey.

They clinked, then downed half of the liquid in the glass. She kept going, drinking till her throat burned and her gag reflex kicked in. She ignored her friends' worried eyes and wished the loud music had started up, but that didn't start until after nine so talking would be on Shey's agenda. Georgia couldn't face that without something less diluted. She rose to get another round in. This time shots.

'I'll help,' Eloisa offered, but Georgia shook her head.

'Same again? I'm moving onto something else.'

'Take it easy,' Shey said.

'Right,' she replied, but it wasn't in agreement.

She made her way through the throng surrounding the bar. It was going to be a nightmare getting served. Spying a gap in the line at the far end of the stretch of servers, she headed straight for it. The bartender took his time making his way to her, despite the fact she clasped a fifty in her hand in plain sight.

To pass the time, she checked out who was there tonight. Maybe Shey was right. Perhaps finding a distraction would take her mind off Max. There were a few potentials, dressed sharp and only sipping at beers instead of downing them. Maybe even the guy with the dark hair a few tables down.

He smiled at her and Georgia returned the gesture. Not wanting to come across as too keen, she turned her back on him, making sure to sway her hips a little in the process. Now he was hooked, she was sure of it. So why did ice suddenly line her stomach? Shit.

She turned, intent on getting out of the way of the guy she'd flirted with. Even caught him rising from the chair from the corner of her eye. That's when she saw Max. If she'd thought the pain she felt on Monday was extreme, this was way worse. His attention was focused on a pretty brunette who was talking to him, her hand gestures as she spoke completely over the top. There were drinks on the table in front of them like they'd both been there a while and weren't moving anytime soon.

She swayed in her shoes a little, until a warm palm settled on her hips. She jerked her head around.

The guy she'd spontaneously hooked was smiling down at her. 'How about I get you a drink?'

Yeah, she could go ten drinks right now. But not with this guy. He was gorgeous, with big brown eyes and a chiseled jaw. His shoulders weren't narrow, but no way would she be able to rest both her thighs on them in the bedroom. Crap, she had to stop comparing men to Max. Especially since he'd clearly moved on.

'I'm here with friends,' she said, not wanting to lead him on.

'That's cool. We can get to know each other while you get them a round in. I'm Donnelly, by the way.' He led her back to wait in line before she could protest.

When they reached the bar, his arm slipped around her waist again. 'And you are?'

*Disappointed.* Where was the rush of attraction, the thrill of flirting? Was it crushed knowing Max was not even twenty feet away with someone else, or was it because Donnelly wasn't Max?

'I'm Georgia,' she said and forced a smile. Why couldn't she have the flirting? She had to get Max out of her head.

Donnelly reached for a strand of her hair and she had to force her feet to stay put. She didn't want to look at the why's too closely. Still, she darted a glance at Max's table and her heart took off. He was scowling at Donnelly's hand, his jaw clenched hard and his brows down.

Who the fuck did Max think he was? The ass was there with another woman and he was giving Donnelly daggers? Suddenly she was all fired up, and maybe not for the right reasons, but she didn't care. Max was tearing her up inside, worse than anyone ever had.

In that second she wanted payback.

She took Donnelly's hands and wove her fingers through his.

He smiled at her. 'So Georgia, what do you do for a living?'

Stepping closer, she made sure to press as much of her body against him as she could. There was no fire, no adrenaline, none of that lost-to-him fear coursing through her, and it was refreshing. There was anger, but anger she could deal with.

'I'm more interested in hearing about you, Donnelly.'

Georgia painted on her most smoldering look and his throat bobbed. She had him in the bag. Getting what she wanted from him would be so easy. But so... boring.

'Georgia, can I have a word?'

Eloisa's voice snapped her out of her tried-and-tested flirting. Leaving Donnelly panting, she threw an apologetic smile over her shoulder while being dragged to another part of the bar by her so-called friend.

'What?' she snipped.

Eloisa scowled. 'You know damn well what. Who was he?'

She shrugged. 'Just a guy.'

'And Max?' Eloisa puffed out air. 'Why are you fucking up your chances with him?'

Her eyes stung and she struggled to keep a hold on her anger. 'Wanna know why that's never going to happen? He's here with another woman. I've been replaced, in four fucking days, with a skinny brunette!'

Her friend's face paled a few shades, which was hard to do since her skin was porcelain most of the time. 'I'm sorry.'

'You were wrong, I'm not missing anything. He's a bastard looking for a fling and I can't do that with him. What option is there other than moving on? Max doesn't—'

'Georgia, stop,' Eloisa pleaded.

Her friend wasn't looking at her anymore. She stared over Georgia's shoulder. For a crushingly horrible moment she wished it was Donnelly who Eloisa was looking at with something like fear.

'Let her go on, I want to hear the rest.'

His voice was too close. All the blood drained out of her face and she wanted to run so badly. Her feet wouldn't move, though. She couldn't move a thing, not even her mouth.

Eloisa must have noticed the panic in her expression because her internal switch flipped to protective and her scowl came out full force. 'I'm assuming you're the bastard.'

'Apparently,' he answered.

She couldn't wimp out like this, couldn't let him see she was terrified how he'd react. Taking a deep breath, she linked arms with Eloisa and turned to face him. God, he was breathtaking in a white dress shirt and suit trousers. He hadn't been at work, or so she'd thought, but why else would he be wearing what he was?

Not wanting to put it off any longer than she had to, Georgia met his gaze, calling on all the anger and pain which almost crippled her. The mask was back, but his eyes were shadowed with something she didn't understand.

'Max,' she said in greeting, but his name burned on the way out.

'We need to talk.' His reply was clipped, but cool.

Shit, this wasn't going to be good.

'You need to back off,' Eloisa retorted. 'Run along back to your date.'

'*Not* my date. Jen's my father's live-in nurse.' He didn't take his eyes off Georgia.

A lump lodged in her throat and she felt shitty for the performance she'd put on with Donnelly. She'd done that to hurt him like he was hurting her, but he wasn't. Something might have happened to his father and, knowing he did have feelings for her, she'd just given him the equivalent of a punch in the face.

Eloisa looked at her and the protective-friend scowl was replaced by concern. Georgia nodded. She had to apologize and didn't particularly want to do it with an audience. How could she have been such a bitch?

'Not here,' he said, pointedly looking at all the bodies surrounding them.

He led her over to the table he'd shared with Jen. It was empty now except for his beer. A waitress came over with a margarita and a glass of brown liquid – probably bourbon. How did he manage to get table service when she couldn't get a drink waiting in line?

The thought ticked her off, but then she remembered what he'd heard. 'I'm sorry.'

He didn't respond, just pushed her glass closer. She took a sip, wishing a hole would swallow her up already. 'I… seeing you with someone else…' Blinking back the tears, she focused on the olive in her glass and tried again. 'It shouldn't have hurt so much. You made it clear you don't want more than what you offered. Problem is, I can't do the pretend thing. Somewhere over the last week I started to feel things for you I shouldn't.'

He tilted her chin up and she met his warm eyes. He didn't look mad now, he looked happy and sad and confused. 'Same thing happened to me. If I'm honest it goes back farther than that. Anytime I spoke with you, I had to force myself to leave. I wanted to get to know you, Georgia, and I convinced myself it was attraction. Lust.'

Her eyes stung again. Regardless of what his words hinted at, she knew they couldn't be together. 'None of that matters though does it? You don't want anything more than pretend.'

'All I know is letting you go was the hardest thing I've ever done and staying away has almost killed me these last few days. I want to be with you and not just for sex. Seeing you with that guy really drove it home.'

Hope loosened the crushing sensation in her chest, but this couldn't be it. One jealous encounter couldn't change his outlook. 'I got the impression you didn't believe in happy endings.'

Max smiled, but it didn't reach his eyes. 'Maybe you could change my mind.'

Georgia wanted to believe him, but nothing was ever that easy. 'Why the sudden turn around? I don't get it.'

He took her hand in his and the contact sparked through her, bringing her to life and making her feel whole again. Amazing how one little touch could make her feel alive.

The mask he always wore slipped and she could see it now. Want and need, and something that might be love, or the start of it.

'I was scared. My mother died and now my father's killing himself so he can be with her. I don't want to be like him, relying on one person for the rest of my life. I don't want the kind of love that makes living without that person impossible. And I don't want to open myself up to that to face another rejection like with Clarissa. But these last few days without you I've had time to put things in perspective.'

She frowned. 'Still not getting it.'

He raked a hand through his hair. 'I don't have to love like that – so all-consuming. But that doesn't mean I can't share my life with someone.'

Her throat constricted. 'You want to spend it with me?'

Squeezing her hand, he smiled for real this time. 'I don't see why we can't give it a shot.'

Georgia pulled her hand back. 'You didn't know me. You still don't.'

Did he think she was soft in the head? Sure, she wanted to believe his words, believe that he was romantic and had it as bad for her as she had for him, but she couldn't.

'I may not know how you take your coffee, or even your friends' names, but I can learn. What I do know is you're the bravest and strongest person I've ever met. After losing your mother you moved to New York even though you were grieving. Georgia, you built yourself a new family and that takes guts. I know that if you and I spend the rest of our lives together and I go first, you'll have the strength to keep living.'

Her heart thumped erratically and her breath hitched. She watched the honesty in his expression dim until sadness took its place. He wasn't making promises but he also wasn't telling her there were no boundaries. And he did know her in the way that mattered. He saw past the sharp tongue to who she really was and it cracked the walls she'd put around herself – maybe that's why he'd been the only man who'd made her come.

But he'd never love her. He'd never let himself, and regardless of how strong he thought she was, she couldn't spend every day loving someone who'd never love her back.

'If you don't want to see where we can go, I'll understand. I've hardly been reliable so far.'

'I'm sorry, Max. I can't accept what you're offering.'

His face fell and he didn't hide the pain in his eyes.

She felt like she was sinking even though she got up. Turning around and walking away was harder this time, like her blood had been replaced with drying cement. Knowing he was prepared to give her forever was something she hadn't known she'd wanted until now.

Turning it down because he couldn't give her more ripped her to shreds.

# Chapter 10

Max watched her walk away feeling like his heart had been replaced with an icy boulder. Rising, he sent a message to his feet to get them to take him out of there. That was when he caught sight of the fucker who'd had his hands all over Georgia. The guy watched her return to her friends, his friend clapping him on the back after he said something, and Max's eyes narrowed.

No way was he going to let some bastard take advantage of her when she was upset. He ordered another drink and told the barmaid to keep them coming. Max didn't acknowledge her flirting, instead, made his way to the upper level where he could keep an eye on Georgia.

For an age she and her friends stayed at their table and he let them have that time alone, checking out the club and the people. His mind kept drifting to earlier that day, when he'd had lunch with his father. They'd talked through a lot of shit, and he realized now why his father was keeping an eye out on the designers. The same reason Max had propositioned Georgia. His father had known Max would drop Marcello as soon as he'd officially retired. The other designers would lose faith in Briggs unless he could prove it wasn't emotion driving his decision to let Marcello go and they might walk too. His father hadn't wanted Max to be left with nothing when he was gone.

Max had gotten so angry that his father hadn't even had faith in him to do it the right way. He hadn't been proud of his reaction, so he'd walked away to calm down some. It left a shitty taste in his mouth that the last words to his father hadn't been the nicest. Too late now, with both his father and Georgia. All he could do was make sure she was okay for the rest of the night and drink himself numb.

The next time he looked for her he found her on the dance floor, close to her friends but she had her eyes closed and was swaying those lean hips in a way that had the fire from the bourbon ripping a trail down to his groin. Mesmerized, all he could do was watch. Everyone around melted into the background as his focus sharpened on her.

Max wanted to go to her, but that wasn't fair. Not for either of them. He meant what he said, he'd have spent every day with her giving her everything he could, but she didn't want any of it. Wasn't that the story of his life?

When a guy slid in close to her – the same guy she'd flirted with at the bar – his hand fisted so tight around the glass it almost cracked. Her smile was small, the colored lights flashing across her pale skin, but what stopped him from storming down there to make sure she was okay was the determination in her eyes. She was moving on and it was then he realized Georgia was the one in control of the situation.

As the guy leaned down to press his lips to hers, Max couldn't take a second more.

* * * *

*Too soon, it was too soon.*

But Donnelly wasn't giving her a second to think about it. His eyes closed as he brought his head down to meet hers. This was supposed to be about getting over Max, moving on, but her insides recoiled at the thought of kissing someone else. She turned her head at the last minute and caught sight of Max rushing down the stairs.

Her heart raced, but it had nothing to do with the wet lips on her cheek. For a second she thought he might make his way over, push Donnelly out the way and then claim her as his. But he turned and headed for the exit.

She glanced at the upper level of the club which was pretty much empty and realized he'd been watching her, probably watching out for her, and he'd gotten an eye-full of her dancing with someone else a few hours after she'd shot him down.

Donnelly pulled her closer, his lips too near and panic made her push him away. Surprise widened his eyes.

'I'm sorry,' she shouted to be heard over the music, but didn't wait for him to reply.

She turned and pushed her way through the throng of dancers, picking up speed when her heels met the carpet leading to the exit. People were filtering in the doors and checking in their coats. All except Max, who passed a ticket to a woman who handed him his suit jacket a moment later.

Her heart was pounding, her breath coming in pants. She didn't know what she was doing, only that she couldn't let him leave. Not without proving he was the one she wanted, not some guy in the club.

She lost sight of him when he slipped outside, but she followed. On the street she whipped her head around, noticing the queue of people and not much else. Across the road, Max was opening the back door of a black town car and she darted out into the street. A cab pulled around the corner too fast and she lost her footing but quickly righted herself and got out of the way.

That was when he looked at her, his chin dropping with shock and his eyes wide. 'Georgia?'

'It's you, not him. I only want you.' She barreled into him, wrapping her hands around his waist. 'Just you.'

Georgia could hear the hysteria in her voice, knew by running after him she'd accepted what he'd offered and would have to deal with it. The panic drained when his arms came around her.

'You could've been killed. Are you crazy?' His voice was rough, laced with ice and it made her smile.

'Apparently. It's what you do to me.'

He slammed her into the car, his head crashing down and his lips meeting her with force and lust and fear. Georgia's heart hammered against her ribs and she pulled him closer by the hair, ground her pelvis against his and didn't care much that she couldn't breathe.

This carnal, overpowering feeling when she touched him, when they were together, was enough. It had to be enough, because the alternative wasn't possible.

When he broke away to breathe, Georgia said, 'Take me to your place.'

He hesitated. Doubt cracked through the lust and need in his expression. 'What's changed?'

'I realized I don't want anyone else. I don't even want to want anyone.'

Tenderly, he cupped her jaw with his palm. 'You deserve better.'

'Are you turning me down again?' Disappointment colored her voice, and she didn't try to hide it.

Max stared at her for so long, doubt began to creep in.

'No. I'll never turn you down again, but I wanted you to know that you deserve more than I can give you.'

'Will you cheat on me? Will you promise me things you can't deliver?' she asked, knowing he never would. That was enough, it had to be.

'Never, on both counts,' he promised.

Georgia smiled. 'Then take me to your place. We've got wasted time to make up.'

He pulled her into the backseat of the car. Eloisa's advice came back to her and she had the feeling again she was missing something, although he'd told her why he didn't want to get close. He didn't want to have to rely on another person, be so consumed by them that when it ended so did he. And he didn't want to have to deal with more rejection – at least she could properly understand that.

'What are you thinking?' he asked. Though he never stopped touching her the whole way, his eyes were shadowed and wary.

Georgia forced herself to focus on what would happen when they got back, so when she spoke he wouldn't hear the lie. 'I want you inside me, holding nothing back, with nothing between us.'

He smiled, but a second later it was replaced with a frown and a curse. 'I don't have condoms.'

She kissed him and though his lips were stunned at first, he quickly caught up and kissed her back. She shifted to straddle him on the seat, pressing her hips close and feeling just how much he was into it when his erection prodded into her sensitive flesh. They had too many clothes, for her liking.

Pulling away, she caught her breath. 'Do you always use protection?'

A line appeared between his brows. 'Yeah.'

'Me too.' She wriggled her hips against him, causing a moan to slip from them both. 'And I'm on the pill, so we're good to go.'

Something hot flared in his eyes. 'You'd take me at my word?'

She nodded. 'And you'd have to take me at mine, but the proof is in my clutch.'

Grabbing the bag, she tried to undo the clip but he pulled it free and tossed it back on the seat. 'What are you doing?'

When his lips were inches from hers, he whispered, 'Taking you at your word.'

All the way back Georgia's mouth was busy and dry humping him had her closer to the edge than she thought possible. All the way up in the lift, his hands were all over her, fanning the flames until her need became unbearable.

She'd freed his cock before he had the door open and the second he kicked it shut Max tugged her panties down enough that they fell to the floor. She'd barely stepped out of them when he lifted her, wrapped her legs around his hips and pushed her back against the wall.

With her core soaking his erection, she demanded, 'In me, now.'

He reared back, then pushed into her all the way to straining point. She gasped, thrilling at the feeling of him filling her to bursting, and that her nerve endings seemed to tingle all over.

'Honey, I've dreamed about this for over a year.' He panted, pressed his forehead against the side of her neck. 'Even the most intense dreams don't cover how fucking right this feels.'

Her heart swelled as she threaded her fingers through his hair. She knew exactly what he meant. 'Max, I need…'

She was going to say him, but couldn't. If this was going to work she had to hold back as much as he did, or she'd end up getting crushed.

He lifted his head and smiled. 'I know.'

What started fast and frantic continued lazily. His lips met hers as his hips rocked into her, stroking deep and making her shiver with each slide over the bundle of nerves inside. She ground into him, digging her heels into his ass to try to rush him on but Max didn't hurry.

Every thrust made her more exhilarated, every drugging kiss racking up the smoldering heat. When her orgasm hit, it stole her breath, but Max didn't stop. He kept up the lethargic rolls of his hips, keeping her pressed tight against the wall, taking her mouth with his. With his hands in her hair, his tongue in her mouth and his erection lodged deep inside, he owned her. Every part of her. That thought sent her over the edge again.

* * * *

Having Georgia naked, in his arms and in his bed eased him more than anything he could remember. Her breathing was deep, feathering across his pecs on the exhale and filling him with purpose and warmth like nothing else. Now she was with him, finally, everything he'd feared for the last few months – hell probably since his mother died – was put in perspective.

She stirred, smiling lazily up at him and his heart swelled.

'Hey,' he said, tucking a strand of hair behind her ear.

'What time is it?' she asked, then yawned.

He checked his watch. 'Almost midnight.'

'I should probably go home.'

She made to move but he held her tighter. 'Stay. Spend the night with me.'

Her frown spiked his adrenaline, or maybe that was fear. She opened her mouth but he cut her off. 'Your friends know where you are, you text them. They must approve, since I haven't heard your cell go off.'

Georgia bit her lip, like she was hiding something and wasn't sure whether to tell him.

'Spill it.' She released her lip and he smoothed the flesh with his thumb. 'You can tell me anything.'

'Will you tell me anything, if I asked?' She met his eyes with curiosity and challenge.

Max waited for the feeling of panic to come, but nothing did. Letting his honesty shine through, he said, 'Yeah. I won't lie to you. Ever.'

She nodded. 'Shey doesn't approve. She thinks I'll end up getting hurt. Eloisa wants me to go after what I want. She thinks that's the only way I'll be happy.'

The idea he would hurt her made it feel like icy fingers were constricting his heart. 'What do you think?'

She threw a leg across his hips, then shifted so she straddled him. Her warm, soaked core – a reminder of all their earlier orgasms – made it hard to concentrate. Especially as blood arrowed south, thickening his too-eager cock.

'I'm swaying toward agreeing with Eloisa.'

A wicked smile curved her lips as she rubbed her core the length of his cock. The tease. In one quick move he shifted their positions so she was trapped below him, completely at his mercy.

'Don't make me restrain you. You might not like it.'

Her eyes flashed with undiluted lust and he almost groaned. Of course she'd fucking like it. If he believed in fate he'd believe she was his other half. His soul mate.

'Max, will you tell me something?'

Her voice, so breathy and sexy, tugged at his wavering control. 'Anything.'

'You said you dreamed about me. Was there... anything in particular you wanted to do when you had me?'

He grinned down at her, pinned her arms above her head in one hand, and kept his other on the bed for support. Grinding his hips so his dick slid across her clit send a shiver of heat down his spine. 'How long have you got? It's a long list.'

Georgia's eyes darkened. 'What's at the top?'

He hesitated, wondering if that would freak her out, but he'd promised to answer. 'I want to claim you, every part of you, every way I can.'

Her eyes widened.

'But we don't have to do that tonight. We don't have to do that ever,' he added, trying to reassure her.

'I'm not ready for... that. I've never...' Her cheeks turned pink.

'I know.' He dropped a kiss on her lips, wishing he hadn't fantasized about having her every way he could. Wishing he could possess her body that way when it obviously made her uncomfortable. 'Want to know my second?'

She nodded.

'I want to tie you up, make you come so many times with my lips and tongue and fingers until you beg me to stop.' Just thinking about it made his cock throb.

'That's hardly fair to you.'

He grinned. 'I've been having orgasms since I was thirteen. It'll take a while for you to catch up, but I'm up to the challenge.'

Georgia lifted her head and he met her mouth halfway, drowning in the feel and taste of her. She pulled away too quickly, a little smile curving her lips.

'I believe you are, but right now I just want you inside me. Wild, hot and crazy.'

Max didn't have to be asked twice. He fucked her with abandon, relishing in the clench of her body every time she came. By the time the sun came up, he'd had her five more times in all the positions he could get her into. As they lay wrapped in sweaty limbs drifting out of consciousness, he knew he could spend the rest of his life doing this with her. In fact, he'd never wanted anything more.

* * * *

Almost a week had passed since Georgia had decided to throw caution to the wind, and hell if it didn't feel sore. She spent most nights with Max and it showed in the perma-smile she couldn't get rid of. Shey had warned her to be careful, but was ultimately happy that she was.

And to make things even sweeter, Max had given her free reign in the store again. They had a dinner to attend that night and she'd picked up a dark-emerald dress that matched her eyes and couldn't wait for him to see her in it.

Eloisa helped with her hair, pulling it into an elegant twist, while Shey gave her a manicure that perfected the look. There were no nerves waiting for Max to pick her up this time and when Eloisa buzzed him up Georgia didn't insist on meeting him outside.

'Be nice,' she warned them both, but knew they'd give him the inquisition of his life. It's why she loved them.

Shey rolled her eyes, a small smile on her lips. Eloisa's look was intense and made Georgia feel like she was on the stand or something. When she raised her eyebrows in question, her friend shook her head, ruffling her auburn curls.

Before she had time to worry what was going on, Max knocked on the door. She almost skipped down the hall and pulled it wide.

His eyes grew huge as he took her in from head to toe.

'You're stunning,' he said.

Georgia eyed the black well-tailored suit he wore and her eyes snagged on the emerald tie. She grinned. 'We match.'

His lips kicked up at the corner. 'I kept tabs on what you bought so I didn't clash with you. I hear girls hate that.'

Her smile grew wider as she heard Shey and Eloisa laugh.

Max offered them a nod, then his eyes were back on her. 'Are you going to invite me in?' he asked, low enough so it was only her who heard.

She stood aside to let him enter, then followed him down the hall. After introducing him properly and dealing with a few mild questions from them both, she wanted to get out but then Shey had to ruin it.

'You know if you hurt her, we've got a rusty knife in the drawer just waiting to be introduced to your balls.'

Georgia scowled at her, remembering when Eloisa had made a similar threat to Calvin. It wasn't fair she was taking it out on Max.

He responded by wrapping an arm around Georgia's waist. 'If I hurt her I'll take it to my own balls.'

She swallowed hard against the lump in her throat. The love that swelled through her was too terrifying she couldn't even take pleasure in her friends' stunned expressions. 'We're going to be late,' she said, tugging his arm.

Max did the goodbye thing while she was too busy fighting for composure. She'd gone and done it. Fallen in love. With a man who'd never love her back.

'You okay?' he asked when they reached the lobby, tugging her hand gently to stop her.

Fighting the turmoil inside, she met his eyes and forced a smile. 'Why wouldn't I be?'

His frown told her he didn't appreciate the evasion, but he didn't push.

'We're going to be late,' she said again and headed for the glass doors.

Max followed, keeping a hold of her hand, but she felt no comfort touching him now. She was too cold. Terror crept in as her future flashed before her in startling HD. She was in love with a man who'd never love her back. She'd given her heart to someone who'd never treasure it like he should.

And leaving him… Pain stabbed through her chest as sharply as a knife. Yeah, leaving him would tear her apart.

# Chapter 11

Georgia was anything but fine. Her hand was cold and clammy in his and she'd gone into some kind of autopilot as they mingled with his designers. Max's stomach shifted uneasily. After what he'd done today, refusing to renew Marcello's contract, he'd counted on her being as open with him as she had been all week, so when she found out she wouldn't think he'd been using her.

He led her through the restaurant to the table where most of them had gathered. His space was at the head, where his father normally sat, and he'd made sure to save her a seat to his right. Pulling out her chair, he shot her a worried look and she smiled a little but didn't meet his eyes.

Fuck, had she found out already? He should have told her, especially since it was likely to come up tonight. Taking hold of her hand, he slid into his chair and ignored every other person in the room. Georgia made small talk with a French woman who he'd just signed to replace Marcello's evening-wear line. His heart thumped uneasily as he realized she could give him away, before he had a chance to explain.

The first course arrived but the chatter didn't die down. What would be hot on the runway at Fashion Week was the topic of the night, and since some of his designers had sets, Max should be spurring them on. Ass-kissing like his father did. Having men and woman that talented signed to only showcase their work in Briggs Department Stores put them ahead of the game, but none of that mattered when Georgia pushed her food around her plate.

She had to know, and he should have been the one to tell her.

'Georgia,' he said quietly. 'Come to the terrace, we need to talk.'

Glancing around, she could see what he could. Everyone was so engrossed in their conversations they wouldn't notice. They slipped away, walking side by side until he parted the French doors and let her walk out ahead of him. It was already dark, and he didn't know if there was a chill in the air or if it was the impending conversation making him cold.

'What's up Max?' she asked, forcing a smile that seemed to strain her lovely face.

His heart pounded painfully. 'I have something to tell you. I didn't want you to hear from someone else.'

* * * *

A million bad-case scenarios ran through her mind, tightening her throat and making it hard to speak. She just stared at him, waiting for the swift and final kick that would put her on her ass. Since she realized how she really felt, a dark cloud had settled over her. A feeling that this was the beginning of the end. Sort of like when she found out her mom was sick.

Georgia didn't think she could go through it again, even with her support system.

Max ran a hand through his hair and blew out a breath. 'I fired Marcello.'

She opened her mouth to respond but couldn't speak. If that's all he had to say, he wouldn't look so agitated. Shifty, even.

'Before, when I wanted to ask you to pretend to be with me, it was a cover.' He paused, trying to let his words sink in, but her mind was numb. 'Georgia, that's not how it is now. It's not why I wanted you, why I still want you. I don't want this to drive a wedge between us.'

Her heart took off, right on cue with her anger. 'You… used me.'

He shook his head. 'No. I asked you to pretend so I'd be able to fire Marcello and make sure the other designers didn't think I did it out of revenge. They'd then start to talk, wonder if it was worth renewing contracts with Briggs now that my dad's out of the picture. But I do care about you, Georgia.'

His lies, her feelings, all the turmoil, all the spilling her guts to him when even now he never spoke about what really mattered to her, screwed with her head. She backed toward the door to the restaurant. Max grabbed her around the waist, pulling her so close she could feel the frantic beat of his heart against hers.

'Georgia talk to me, don't fucking leave.'

The desperate plea in his voice didn't melt her anger, it only made it hotter. She pushed at his chest but he didn't budge. 'You made me fall for you on a lie.'

His jaw dropped. 'No, we were never a lie. I've always told you the truth.'

She shook her head, mostly to try and clear it. 'A lie by omission is still a lie.'

Her voice broke and her eyes stung. Where the hell was rage when she needed it?

'Shit, Georgia. Don't be upset. I'm sorry. I should have told you.'

She pushed at his chest again, but he crushed her to him. 'Believe this.'

His lips were on her before she could take a breath, desperate and hungry. Her traitorous body responded, warming, heating, opening, for him. When his tongue forced its way into her mouth, tears streamed from her eyes and she'd done what she'd swore never to do. Fallen for someone who couldn't love her, couldn't even be honest with her. She was crying, sobbing, and wishing things were so different. But she knew what she had to do.

Anger at herself for being so weak pulsed through her. She bit his tongue as hard as she could and he flinched away, muttering a curse.

'I never want to see you again!' She backed away to the door while he watched her with that shuttered expression she hated.

Forcing back a sob, she turned and pulled the door open. Georgia ignored the fact that all eyes were on her. She grabbed her bag and made her way to the front of the restaurant, asking one of the waiters to call her a cab. She was outside, breathing through her nose to hold back the pain when he caught up with her.

'What the fuck was that?'

Georgia whirled, not caring if he saw how angry and upset she was. His face paled. 'That was me saying it's over. That was me telling you I'm not working for Briggs anymore. That was me showing you I can't be with you the way you want me to be.'

'Georgia think about this. What we have—'

'We have nothing! I can't deal with loving someone who lies to me, someone who uses me, someone who can't love me back!' She didn't even care that the people on the streets could hear. Some part of her noted she was crazy, and losing more of her mind every second she waited on the damn cab.

He stepped closer but she held her hand up. 'Don't, just don't. I can't be near you, Max. It hurts too much.'

A yellow cab pulled up in front of the building and she slipped in, not looking back. Clutching her aching chest, she mumbled her address to the driver and told him to hurry. She needed her family and she needed to move on with her life for good. No looking back and no more taking chances.

* * * *

Max didn't know what time it was when he pulled up outside his father's apartment. He hadn't seen him for days, but had no one else to turn to. His heart was possibly broken. Every ounce of energy in him had been drained out, and when he rested his head against the leather seat, his eyes slid shut.

A knocking woke him up from the nightmare. Shivering and soaked through, he almost sighed in relief until he saw Jen through his windshield. It hadn't been a dream, then. Georgia had really left him and going by the early morning light he'd fallen asleep in his car.

He got out, shaking his head at Jen's worried expression. Vaulting the steps two at a time, he let himself into his father's home and headed straight for the bedroom. A clattering in the kitchen caught his attention and, frowning, he made his way toward the sound.

His father was mixing stuff in a bowl when he reached the room and Max's jaw dropped. He looked stronger, a little healthier around his face and nothing like the skeleton he'd taken everything out on not even a week ago.

'Dad?' he asked, making sure this wasn't another dream.

'Just in time for pancakes. Remember your mother used to make them with chocolate chips? I've almost perfected the recipe.' His father dumped a bag of chocolate bits into the mixture then kept on whisking.

'What's going on?' he asked.

Maxton turned to him with a smile, which froze in place as his gaze reached his son: 'What happened? You look like hell.'

He raked a hand through his hair, still damp with sweat. 'And you don't.'

Leaving the bowl on the granite counter, he slid into a chair at the table. 'Sit. Talk to me.'

Looking down at his father, he couldn't get his head around the difference. Maxton didn't just look healthier; he'd put on much-needed weight. In four fucking days, he'd bounced back. Sure, he was still thin but this was more than he could ever hope for.

'What's going on?' he asked again.

Maxton's eyes brimmed over with tears. 'I miss her, Max. So much it's hard just to get out of bed in the morning, but last week was the wake-up call I needed.'

He winced, remembering every hateful word he'd slung.

'Don't regret what you did. It's what I needed to hear. I'll get to be with your mother again one day, but I have others I care about here. Others who need me.'

Max slumped into a chair across from him, his head supported on his hands, covering his face. 'I'm sorry. I was so angry. Selfish. I shouldn't have—'

'Son, I was the selfish one, and I shouldn't have doubted you knew what you were doing with the business. I know it's going to take more than an apology to put things right, but I'm going to try.'

Max lifted his head and all he saw was sorrow and honesty. He wanted to smile, wanted to reassure, but fuck if he could move a muscle. His face was numb while his emotions tore him in two.

'Max, talk to me. You look like your life's just ended.' There was no escaping the worry in his father's eyes, and no holding in the truth.

'I hurt Georgia, bad.'

His father frowned. 'Tell me everything, from the beginning.'

Max did, shame curdling his insides with every disapproving look. He'd fucked it up with her beyond repair. Admitting the whole sorry thing to his father didn't make him feel better. It only heightened the end-of-the-world feeling he'd been sporting since she told him she never wanted to see him again.

When he was done, Maxton was quiet for a long time. He couldn't meet his father's gaze. Shame burned through him along with the fear and the pain. Shit, even when Clarissa had humiliated him it didn't feel a thing like this.

'I never thought I'd live to see the day when you disappointed me, son.'

His throat constricted and his shoulders slumped. 'I...'

'I also never thought I'd see the day when you missed the obvious. You were always such a smart kid.'

He met his father's eyes with a frown. 'What do you mean?'

Maxton shook his head, a smile curving his lips. 'You've spent so long convincing yourself you can't fall in love because you're so scared of rejection. But all along you've been falling hard.'

Max ground his teeth, rejecting the idea even though the proof that there was strength to be found after loss was sitting right in front of him. He couldn't imagine that kind of grief, tearing him up. But then his own rocked him to the core with startling clarity and his mouth fell open.

'And you said it yourself, she loves you to the point that she can't bear to be with you since you told her you can't. I don't think you have to worry about Georgia screwing you over.'

'I… oh God.' He buried his face in his palms again. He didn't think Georgia would leave him the way Clarissa did, but there were other ways a person could leave. Only question left was did he take that chance and risk getting fucked over, or go after what he wanted?

A scrape of a chair sounded, then his father's palm rested against his shoulder, stronger than he expected. 'You've got a lot of making up to do, son. Go get yourself cleaned up.'

He shook his head. 'I've messed up.'

Maxton patted him on the back. 'Maybe. You'll never know that until you admit how you feel to yourself, then prove it to her.'

Max's arms shook and he groaned. Shit wasn't supposed to happen like this. He wasn't meant to fall for a woman, but how could he deny it now?

It meant nothing, though. Without Georgia, none of it mattered – which was what he'd been worried about happening – but if there was a chance to fix this, how could he not try?

'You can't sit there all day. Aren't you going to try and win her back?' his father asked.

Wasn't that the million-dollar question?

# Chapter 12

A very unwelcome Shey stormed into her room and Georgia pulled the covers over her head.

'When are you going to get out of this hovel and get your act together?'

Never wasn't long enough. She was bleeding, torn, betrayed and fucking hurt. What did her friends expect? At least Eloisa had the good grace to leave her alone, though that was probably because of the mess. She'd shit a hedgehog if she had to spend any time in Georgia's room.

'It's Sunday,' she mumbled. 'There's no point getting out of bed.'

The mattress dipped under Shey's weight. 'What about tomorrow? You have a job.'

She shook her head under the covers, but Shey pulled them back. 'You stink by the way. A shower wouldn't kill you, you know.'

'Leave. Me. Alone.' Georgia put the last of her energy into a scowl that should have had Shey shaking in her stilettos.

'Believe me, I want to. I won't though. Not until you get your act together.'

Irritation bubbled over. 'Maybe I don't want to!'

'How are you going to pay for food, for rent, for clothes?' she demanded.

She turned to face the wall. 'I have savings.'

'Right, I've had enough of this shit.'

Georgia exhaled a sigh of relief, until Shey caught both her ankles. 'What are you doing?'

'If you're not getting out of this bed, I'm going to make you. Then I'm getting Eloisa in here and we're going to lock you in the bathroom till you're clean. Just imagine how tidy your room will be when Eloisa gets her way, then you'll never be able to find anything.'

She stared hard into her friend's unwavering golden gaze, until she realized Shey wasn't bluffing. 'Fine. I'll go take a frickin' shower.'

Shey released her and she rose, pulling her towel off the radiator. 'Remember the soap.'

'You should have been a comedian,' Georgia grumbled, making her way to the bathroom. Her body was stiff, but a weekend in bed would do that. She ignored the mirror and scrubbed herself from head to toe, feeling a teeny bit better by washing away the grime, though she hated to admit her friend was right.

Still felt like a bullet had split her ribcage, and she was bleeding out, but whatever. She was clean and Shey wasn't following through on her threat. When she got back to the room she scowled, seeing the sheets had been changed. Pulling on sweats and a hoodie, she was tempted to slide back into bed, but that would just earn her more threats.

Instead she padded barefoot through to the living room, wondering why the apartment was so quiet. On the coffee table there was a card with her name on the front in Eloisa's handwriting.

She flipped it open and frowned at the words.

*You don't have long. Slap your war paint on and wear something sexy. I'll keep Shey away as long as I can.*

She read over the note again and again, trying to make sense of it, wishing the conclusion she came to was the wrong one. Since she'd got back on Thursday night and broken down for the first time since her mom died, Shey had cussed Max out over and over. Come Friday night Georgia had locked herself in her room, half-agreeing with Shey and half-hating her friend for speaking about Max the way she had. Eloisa had offered comfort, but hadn't said a bad thing about him. Not once.

Georgia had a sinking feeling she'd been set up. She ran through to her bedroom, scrambling to find her handbag and pulled out her phone. Finding a charger amidst the chaos of her room drove home the fact that she needed organization in her life. The second it was plugged in she switched it on.

The piece of crap took forever to load up.

No missed calls. No voicemails. Her heart broke all over again, but it didn't make sense. She hit out a text to Eloisa.

*What's going on?*

The reply came back within second.

*You can thank me later x*

Georgia frowned at the screen.

*For what?*

The sound of the front door opening had her straightening up. She left her phone in her room, wondering what the hell her roomies were up to now. Walking down the hall, she said 'I thought you two wouldn't be back for a while.'

When she saw him standing in the living room, she had to palm the wall for support. Movement caught her eye and she gaped at the people strolling into her apartment with huge bouquets of flowers, laying them on every available surface till her apartment smelled absolutely gorgeous.

Max didn't move throughout, but she felt him watching her. Stunned, she couldn't speak, even when the last person left. He didn't have keys to her place. There was only one person he could have got them from. Someone she trusted, someone she loved. Eloisa's betrayal turned her stomach.

'You look how I feel,' he said.

Anger pulsed through her veins, warming her, focusing her. 'Like shit? Good. You deserve to.'

He shook his head, his blond hair falling into his face.

'Devastated, miserable, cut to shreds.'

'You're giving yourself far too much credit.' Thank God she had her wayward tongue. He looked too good in jeans and a sweatshirt. Even with the empty eyes.

'Yeah, maybe.' He pushed his hair out of his face. 'It's how I felt when you walked away from me on Thursday, but I didn't know why right away.'

Could this get any worse? Him surrounded by the flowers he'd bought her, given access to her home by her so-called-friend, saying he wanted her back? Really?

'Flowers won't change anything.' Even if they were pretty and romantic. 'I thought I made myself clear on Thursday.'

'You did. You made everything crystal clear.'

She blinked a few times, not sure what was happening.

'You made it clear you loved me, and that you couldn't stay with me because you thought I'd never love you back.'

Hearing that made the pain hit her again. She leaned against the wall, feeling like her knees were about to fail. He was in front of her in an instant, but she shook her head. She wouldn't survive it if he touched her again, she was sure of it.

'Jesus, Georgia. When was the last time you ate?' His voice was thick with worry.

She couldn't bear it. Closing her eyes she said, 'You need to go.'

'I'm not leaving until you hear me out.'

Her forehead crumpled. 'There's nothing more to say. This doesn't change anything, or what you did.'

He picked her up so quickly she only had time to gasp. In his arms, cradled against his chest, was a special kind of torture. She yearned for it, almost needed it, but he was moving and a second later sitting her on the armchair.

Kneeling before her, he held onto the arms of the chair, his expression more pained than she'd ever seen it. 'I was wrong, Georgia. I need you. I've fallen in love with you and was too scared to see it.'

She shook her head back and forth, breathing through her nose, trying to stop the burning in her eyes.

'Georgia, I know you think I was using you to make breaking Marcello's contract seem like the end of his time, rather than revenge. I'll admit I did need someone to help me out when I thought about asking you, and should have come clean, but then I fucked up by asking you to sleep with me too and lost my chance.'

'You should have told me. When I asked about Clarissa, that was your chance.' He hadn't, though. He'd pushed her away.

Max buried his face in her lap and she was torn between comforting him and shoving him away. Instead she fisted her hands at her sides.

'I was running scared. Pushing you away because I couldn't deal with how you were making me feel. It wasn't till that day at the hospital that I realized how much I needed you. At the time it freaked me out, seeing what love was doing to my father. And then knowing from personal experience what being cheated on by someone I cared about felt like.'

He lifted his head and begged her to understand with his eyes.

She couldn't. 'Then tell me what's changed? You were prepared to walk away from me after that. Hell, you've waited days to come here.'

He took one of her hands in his and her heart swelled with hope, but she pulled it back. Believing in them again for it all to come crashing down would end her.

'I talked with my father. Really talked. He's on the mend, I'm not angry at him anymore, and he got me to face my love for you.'

A sob slipped out. Before she knew it she was in his arms, straddling his hips when he'd switched positions, and clinging onto him like she couldn't bear to let go. 'This… isn't me. I don't… cry,' she said between sobs.

'I know, honey. Eloisa told me. I was ready to hand them my balls and let them stick the knife in, but she gave me an in. A shot to prove how much I care.'

'I can't go through another split again. I can't deal with it.' She looked him in the eye, showing him how serious she was.

His hands cupped her face. 'I know. I can't either.'

He kissed her then and the suffering ended. Georgia kissed him back, reveling in the beat of her heart, the blood pumping thick and hot through her body. He'd been right all along, he knew what she needed. Him, pure and simple.

Max lifted her off the chair and she wrapped her arms around his neck. They were moving, but all she could focus on was his erection, hot and heavy at her core. Need melted her insides, boiling hot, until he took his lips off hers and she realized where they were.

*Oh, hell.*

'Umm…' She had no defense against the mess, the chaos.

He laughed and the sound vibrated through her enough to clear the shock. 'I didn't expect anything else.'

The way he smiled at her, with adoration and total acceptance, made her heart swell. 'The sheets are clean.'

Two steps were all it took for him to reach the bed and he fell back against the mattress so she straddled his hips. He pulled her hoodie over her head, exposing her naked torso. His blue eyes turned stormy, sending a thrill through her.

Shifting, she managed to ditch the bottoms. He rolled them both, his lips fixing onto her breast, stoking the flames inside. 'Max!' Her hands fisted in his hair, pulling him closer. 'Get naked.'

He switched his attention to her other breast while his fingers found her clit. Jolts of pleasure muddied her thoughts. She let go of his hair to claw at the sheets, and he trailed his lips down to her core.

'I've missed you. Everything about you.' His tongue lashed between her folds and he growled as she whimpered. 'Fuck, your *taste.*'

He utterly devoured her, sending her straight over the edge in one fast, hot, wild orgasm. When his mouth didn't let up, she found the strength to reach for him and tug his hair. When his head lifted, a fresh wave of heat pulsed through her seeing his shiny lips.

'I want you. In me. Now.' Because love wasn't just about giving, or taking. It was about both, simultaneously, and she wanted him to experience that with her.

Max kneeled, pulling his sweatshirt over his head while she unbuttoned his jeans. It only took a few seconds for him to kick them off, and less time for him to get between her thighs and slide home. Georgia relished in the stretch, digging her nails into his ass to pull him closer. All the while his eyes fixed on hers, shining with ecstasy and love.

Max made love to her slowly, savoring and giving, while she squeezed around him and told him exactly how much she loved him. When they both came, he collapsed on top of her and she lay wrapped around him, in his arms and still speared by him.

'I don't want you to leave,' he finally said.

'I can't, not now. You're a part of me.'

He lifted his head, his smile blinding. 'You're the best part of me, honey.' After a second his brow creased. 'Will you come back to work? We don't have to tell anyone if you don't want them to know.'

'I don't care what they know. I can handle gossip. But I can't handle you keeping more secrets from me.'

'There's nothing else,' he swore. 'You know more about me than anyone.'

'That'll do. For now.' She closed her eyes, a peaceful kind of exhaustion closing in.

Max shifted them so they were on their sides, still not breaking their connection. 'I swear to you, I won't hold back anything else.'

'I believe you,' she whispered.

Max pulled her close, feeling his warmth and love seep in through her pores. She drifted to sleep knowing he would be there when she woke up. Maybe even for the rest of her life.